ENRAGED BEAST

CONWAY XAVIER

MINERVA PRESS
MONTREUX LONDON WASHINGTON

ENRAGED BEAST

ISBN 1 85863 353 2

First published 1994 by
MINERVA PRESS
10 Cromwell Place
London SW7 2JN

Printed in Great Britain by
Martins the Printers Ltd., Berwick upon Tweed

ENRAGED
BEAST

ABOUT THE AUTHOR

As a mature student Conway Xavier studied English at Ruskin College, Oxford and then at Wadham College, Oxford.

After leaving full-time education he obtained a teaching position and recently gained an MSc. in politics.

He is currently head of English at a sixth form college and is researching for his doctorate in the field of industrial relations.

To all those people who are
desperately trying to survive the recession

Chapter 1

A young man closed the front door behind him and stood for a moment on the pavement. He blinked in the startlingly bright Saturday morning sunshine and mumbled:

"I feel like bloody Dracula at bloody dawn."

It was 11.30am and as was common at that time each week he was hung-over. The sunshine burned his eyes.

"Still, nothing for it, hair of the bloody dog time again."

He started to walk down the hill, eyes fixed to the ground, averting the brief glances of passing people.

Having reached the age of 22 he had spent the last eight years drinking and, whilst other desires had been tasted and exploited to the full, he had yet to conquer the after-effects of a heavy Friday night session. He passed the bill-board on the corner which had a poster advertising some new breakthrough in dental treatment. He was not particularly impressed and his eyes stared fractiously at the offending message.

"Bloody scientists working on bloody teeth should have invented a bloody cure for a bloody hang-over," he growled, emphasising each 'bloody' with an imaginary point of an aggressive finger towards an imaginary scientist.

He took the long way round to the pub, passing the newsagents where he could buy a bottle of milk and a wedge of cornish pasty.

"Line me stomach before the first pint and get a bit of ballast inside of me," he thought, in a manner which spoke of years of practice.

Sitting on the wall by the car park opposite the newsagents and cramming the pasty into his mouth he washed it down with slurps of milk.

"That's bloody better" he commented, "and now for a pint."

Although a drinker by nature Victor Manning had none of the cliched down-at-heels habits of the stereotypical drunk. He was smartly dressed in his dark blue suit and cleanly polished brogues. His shirts were ironed and fashionable. His dark hair was short and brushed and slightly damp from the dowsing he had given it that morning. His face however betrayed a rougher side to his character. Dark of complexion for an Anglo-Saxon, he had the looks that in the fifties would have made for a perfect Hollywood gangster; born out of his time, he could have rivalled Cagney in 'White Heat'. His eyes adapted chameleon like to the joys, passions and hatreds which dominated his life. If they were the reflection of his soul then his soul was intense, dark and threatening. It was only after several pints that his eyes lost their expressiveness and assumed the monotonous glaze of a session drinker.

He reached the Lamb and Flag just on noon and pushed open the door.

"Morning, Victor," the landlord greeted him, in an open and chatty manner. "Pint of Master Brew?"

"Nope, I'll have Bishop's Finger today and make it two, the first one ain't gonna touch me bloody throat."

He watched the landlord pour the beer from a hand pump and then gazed ardently as the beer swirled and settled in the glass. While the second drink was being drawn Victor took the pint and his large hand closed round the glass. Raising it to his lips he drank in large gulps, dribbling small rivulets down each side of his mouth. In nine seconds it was gone.

"Bloody shock tactics." Victor explained. "Treat the first like a bloody blitzkrieg of panzer tanks. It soon kicks the bloody stomach into action. By the way, what happened to that bloke last night?"

"What, the one you used his head for football practice with? I don't know and I don't care. He isn't a regular and he was getting too out of hand. Been drinking for most of the day it seems. Still, if he can't learn not to throw abuse at the wrong people he's going to have to learn pretty quick."

Trouble had occurred when one drunk had decided to take Victor on in an argument. It had turned heated with the drunk threatening violence. Like most drunks the words were not matched by coordinated fists and Victor had thrown him out of the pub and finished him off on the street. He had left him collapsed by a lamp post with a small pool of blood slowly circling his head, outlining the profile like a macabre silhouette. One of the passers-by had phoned for an ambulance which had taken about ten minutes to arrive. What happened after that neither Victor nor the landlord knew. The police would treat it as another typical Friday night in a Medway Towns pub and would quietly forget the incident. It had been a lousy end to what had been quite a good day. The previous afternoon Victor had gone to Dartford to try and buy into a local video shop. His own series of shops were in central and South Kent and he was looking to expand. So, he and one of his partners, Dave, had opened negotiations with the owner and they were proceeding quite nicely, the only rival being an operation from London. He'd left Dave to continue the negotiations the next day while Victor returned to Rochester, to beer, to a Friday night session, and to a Saturday morning hangover.

Victor took his second pint and sat down in a mahogany walled corner that had, by common consent, become his corner. His eyes assumed a neutral stare as he surveyed the familiar interior of the pub.

It was an old building, built over two hundred years ago to accommodate the growing trade from the then thriving docks. Its walls retained much of their original panelling and the pub kept the traditional three bar division: the public bar for the workers complete with pool table dartboard and juke box; the saloon bar for the blokes with their girlfriends, and the small snug bar for the old dears. As the docks declined and the workers moved away so the pub gradually fell into a form of dignified crumbling seediness like some ageing has-been still trying to relive former glories. It became, like so many others in the area, a place insular in its atmosphere, serving its regulars but frowning on strangers and facing the future with an exterior which bore all the scars of the past. It needed to be refurbished or closed down but it made too little money for the former and too much for the brewery to do the latter. It survived. Apart from the landlord there was nobody else in the public bar, not uncommon for an area where the number of pubs far exceeded demand.

This part of Rochester, the small village of Troy Town, was guarded over by a regiment of pubs. Most existed on a regular set of drinkers; few were adventurous enough to provide anything other than an atmosphere of claustrophobic hostility.

Like an institution in decline the pubs had substituted past excellence for a desperate and dull present. It had been fortunate that the new landlord of the Lamb and Flag was not from Rochester. He had come up from Faversham and had brought with him a taste for proper beer. As such the pint at the pub had improved in quality. It had started to draw in the evening drinkers but still not enough to ensure its continued survival. It could, like other pubs in the area, be closed at any moment, and this insecurity had goaded the landlord into experimenting with differing forms of entertainment. He had brought in a local band, but they had proved to be too expensive; he had tried pub quizzes and had a regular team in the league, but this had brought in the serious players intent solely on winning and not on drinking; he had even attempted to provide an extensive range of pub food but that had resulted in the food inspector closing down his inadequate and unhygienic kitchen. At last he had stumbled his way towards the old fashioned idea of the pub stripper. His wife had at first frowned upon this, wanting instead to create a family pub, but as the customers started to return and as the receipts started to build up her opposition faded. There was something reliable about this form of entertainment, something Bacchanalian about combining the erotic with alcohol. The stripper, a belly full of fine ale, and then home to slump in front of the tele, formed a kind of trilogy which retained a powerful appeal.

Victor had watched the changes with approval, especially the better quality beer and had started to enjoy the more open atmosphere of this bar.

He was just finishing his second pint and was starting to feel comfortable when his reverie was interrupted by a wellbuilt man standing at his table.

"Hello, Mr. Manning, how are you today?"

"Oh, bloody hell, what do you want now? I told you that I'd got a new import licence, if the customs people were more efficient there wouldn't have been the problem. OK?"

"No problem, no problem, that's been sorted out. Can I buy you a drink?"

"No thanks, being seen drinking with you would really damage my bloody credibility, wouldn't it."

The man drew in a deep breath and, uninvited sat down.

"Still, you don't mind if I join you for a moment, do you? I'd like some information, if you have it. Nothing heavy, something is happening in the video world which you'd be against anyway."

Victor had not expected this line of questions, last night's violence was registering and he was momentarily taken aback. Pausing for a moment before replying, he studiously watched a fly crawl up the window. As this concerned his line of business he was interested.

"OK, Inspector Morse-Sweeney-Taggart, bloody well ask away."

"Right, well, to be blunt, Manning, what I'd like to know is: do you have anything on a child porno ring? You see, some revolting and disgusting videos are being pushed in Kent and the capital. I'm asking all the suppliers if they've come across anything in their travels."

Victor stopped drinking and looked shocked.

"You must be bloody joking. I deal in classy videos, not bloody pervert films."

"Yes we know you do, but I'm just asking if you've heard anything. You see, the reason why I had to investigate your licence the other week was because I've got to investigate a new vice ring which seems to be moving in on your territory. You were the last on my list. Now I know, Victor old lad" the policeman shifted forward on his chair, "that not everything you do is strictly legal."

"Then book me," replied Victor, "and my name's Manning, don't use my first name, you ain't a friend."

"Ah, sorry Mr. Manning. To carry on, we've no intention of booking you, at the moment." He added the last three words with a slow deliberation. "However, I would like to ask some questions."

"Are you trying to lean on me?"

"Yes," came the blunt and quick reply. The tone then changed to a more conciliatory one. "Look, Manning, we know about your set up and your confederates, your partners in crime."

The policeman stared into Victor's eyes provoking an immediate and aggressive defensive reaction.

"Hang on a bloody minute, I ain't saying anything else. If you want to take action then book me and take me down to the station. My group is legitimate."

"All right, all right, I was a bit heavy, but will you just answer one thing? Will you tell me if you have any knowledge of another firm trying to move in on your territory? Have you for instance had a decline in orders over the past few weeks? Have you noticed that any dealers are less favourable towards you than before?"

Victor shook his head to all these questions. He had not noticed anything unusual, except the fact that some orders had declined rather more than expected during the holiday season. He pointed this out to the policeman who took immediate notice.

"What do you mean? I'd have thought sales and rentals go up during the holidays, people have time to watch films."

"Not during the summer holidays, people go out."

"Has it been a general decline or a localised one?"

"A couple of shops," said Victor who was starting to become interested. "I didn't give it a second thought. Some dealers go under because they're bad, some prosper because they're bloody good. I just thought the decline was part of the recession hitting the crap stores."

"It might be, it might be. There may also be a drugs angle to this operation, with the firm shipping in stuff from Europe. Know anything about drugs?"

It was, as he knew a rhetorical question. Victor was an old fashioned dealer, a bit of a wide boy, a little bit dodgy but definitely not into drugs. Victor pursed his mouth and grabbed his pint glass:

"No, I don't know anything about drugs, but as we are now firmly enmeshed in the European quagmire, I suspect that the hardcore porn and the bloody drug market will flourish. What's happening now, free movement across the EEC? No trade or customs barriers? Very good for the gangsters. What are you coppers going to do about it?"

It had been Victor's turn to ask the rhetorical questions and the answers were not lost on the policeman. He avoided them.

"Yes, well, thanks for the political lecture and thanks for your help. Could you do me one last thing and keep your eyes open and let me know if anything comes in on the grapevine as they say."

"Yeah, OK, now if you don't mind pushing off."

Inspector Benjamin got up from his seat and, not bothering to offer his hand in a parting shake he turned and moved towards the door. At the bar he handed a fiver to the barman:

"Put that behind the bar for Victor will you, I owe him a drink."

Benjamin left the pub and was soon back at his desk at Rochester Police Station.

Victor continued to think about what Benjamin had said to him after he had gone. The news that a potential rival had entered the field bothered him just a little. Sipping on his beer he concentrated hard on the possible threat and what to do about it. The concentration meant that the effects of the alcohol went down the 'business passage' as he called it rather than the more pleasant 'relaxation passage'. It would sharpen his thinking and also, to some extent his paranoia. Like many successful men he was always on the look-out for possible threats to his position. However, unlike other paranoid men he did not have the narcissistic tendencies which would isolate him from his group. His world was a limited one of definable targets and realisable aims. In planning the former he was precise and in realising the latter he could be ruthless. Not that there had been any real violence in the pursuit of his interests; just a strong determination to succeed. He lived through a series of contradictions and tensions: both rational and passionate, peaceful and explosive, light and dark. When the two sides of his character were in balance, in a kind of controlled tension he was at his most restrained, when under pressure he could act swiftly and with inexorable single-mindedness. In combination these two aspects of his character contributed to what his friends called his 'ever changing moods'.

Another and more pleasant interruption came to his thoughts as a small and well dressed man in his thirties sauntered up to his table and placed two glasses down:

"I've got the money Victor, he coughed up alright, no problem. He said the videos were perfect, but could we get hold of some of the Danish sex imports next time, violence ain't selling too hot at the moment."

The small man handed over an envelope containing £500.

"I've also spoken to Charlie about the cars and he says that he can have them stripped down in a couple of weeks."

Victor sipped his beer and pocketed the money.

"And I saw Dave yesterday evening and he says..."

"Shove Dave for the moment. What I want to know, Lawyer" he said to the little man, " is, what do you mean he don't want any more violence videos? We've 200 more of the bloody buggers and we've got to shift them. I ain't going to be bloody well stuck with a pile of Rambo/Die Hard/Kung Fu rip offs, not bloody likely. He said three weeks ago that he wanted them. Now what do you mean he wants pervert videos instead?"

"He says they ain't..."

The small man was interrupted by a flash of anger from Victor's eyes. His glance came powerfully like the punch of a fist.

"I don't give a toss what he says, business is business. Either he takes the videos or I'll bloody deal with him. Understand Lawyer I'll bloody deal with him."

The small man knew Victor at these moments and knew that to challenge him was to court danger. Instead of replying he looked into his half pint glass and waited for the moment to pass. He knew it would. Victor's anger came in spurts, over in a second; the trick was to wait for the anger to pass before trying to placate his boss. He'd reported accurately what the video dealer had said and knew that he was angling for a cut-price deal on the remaining films. Knowing he'd have to wait before broaching the subject again he played for time swirling his beer around his glass. Although he ran a small antiques business his real interest was in scrap metal and buying and selling jewellery. For those whom he knew he also acted as a kind of pawnbroker, lending money on precious stones, electrical goods or anything else of value. It was because of this last activity that he had joined the Class, for reasons of protection after one client had come close to wrecking his shop. Victor had been there selling a clapped out motor for scrap and had effectively dealt with the client with one threatened slash of his cut-throat razor. It had been the reflex like action of Victor which had impressed him most and when he was asked whether he could provide an outlet for some of Victor's secondhand video recorders he had readily agreed. Since then he had become more firmly entrenched in the Class, preferring the alcoholic effectiveness of Victor's organisation's protection to the more official but inefficient protection of the police. He became the diplomat of the Class, often dealing with the more touchy of Victor's clients and they called him the Lawyer. Victor was the energy, the strategist and the calculating brains; the Lawyer was the restraining influence.

Chapter 2

The Class was a business and was made up of a loose connection of like-minded people. People who existed in a twilight world of buying short and selling long, of shady deals and the main chance. They were a new type of petty criminal, banded together for common interests and for protection but each offering a particular speciality. Unlike the gangsters of the fifties and sixties, unlike the Krays and the Richardsons, the Class were not interested in empire building. They had no desire to indulge fantasies of being local heroes or of 'keeping the manor quiet'. They did not wish to he seen in the presence of minor stars and has-beens, nor did they control local politicians. They considered these gangsters as being born losers and they had no intention of falling in some tragic and inevitable confrontation with the law. The gangsters of yesterday came out of clearly defined communities and had set their ambitions at being Lord of their manor, of being king for a day, but they ended their careers either splayed out on some city mortuary table or as Punch, the Fool, mocked by those of greater power. There could be no romance attached to these failed gangsters, for ultimately their violence had rebounded against them. As far as possible the Class stayed clear of violence because violence was not profitable.

By now the pub was starting to fill up and was coming to life. The landlord was at his usual place, just by the bar chatting to one of his favourite regulars with his back turned towards the corner whilst the first record from the juke box came on.

"Bloody Stock, Aitken and Waterman again. Artificial rubbish played by rip-off merchants and listened to by wallies."

Victor had finished his second pint and was into his third. The alcohol started to course through his veins, relaxing him and making a faint reddish glow appear on his cheeks. Victor always thought that beer was like a liberating army come to rescue his body from dullness and mediocrity. The similes he used for this were all military, 'bloody panzers' and 'bloody seventh cavalry' being his favourites. The 'bloodies' would soon cease as he replaced his blunt aggressive speech with a lucidity which reflected his intelligence.

"You ought to have gone into the music business Victor and become a star; all those girls, the bright lights, you'd have liked that sort of life." The Lawyer was meandering around subjects now, waiting for the change in Victor's mood which would be the signal for some serious business talk.

He was interrupted by a heavily built man blundering towards their corner. Victor looked up:

"Pete, you look like you've been in a marathon, you're gushing sweat. Sit down before you have a heart attack."

"No time, Victor. We've got to move quick. Dave's been done-over. Some geezers from London are trying to take over our business. They're dumping videos on the local shops, flooding the market. Dave went to see them up in the city and they done him in. We're in trouble, Victor."

Pete dropped into a chair threw back his head and looked upwards towards the ceiling with sweat streaming down his face. His mouth was wide open and he brought a sleeve quickly across his face to mop up the perspiration. Leaning forward he forced a rush of breath through his mouth and slumped his forearms on the table, slightly jolting the Lawyer's half pint glass and causing some beer to slop out. The Lawyer looked at Pete in an exasperated fashion.

"Steady on old son," he said. Pete looked apologetically at the small pool of beer on the table.

As a figure Pete was huge. A combination of strong lager, fast junk food and lack of exercise had slowly ruined his once powerful body, gradually tipping it over into obesity and he smelt permanently of sweat. He was childlike in his short concentration span, not very intelligent and was easily excitable. Pete was the messenger, driver and dogsbody of the Class. Victor ignored the accident and Pete's flustered condition. The news that Dave had been beaten up, combined with the report from the police inspector, hammered into Victor's lively mind, which had now fully awaken from its predrink state of lethargy:

"Lawyer. Get on the phone and get the Class together. We've got some thinking to do. And whilst you're at it, get the beers in."

By 1:30pm the small corner was packed with six people engaged in intense conversation. Around their table was a gap. The pub's regulars had moved towards the makeshift stage at the other end of the bar, anticipating the first dancer and avoiding the conspiratorial group in the corner. The landlord was urging them on with catcalls and shouts. Then a cheer went up from the drinkers as the first dancer appeared and made her way in a self absorbed style towards the stage. The DJ put a record on the turn table and she started her dance.

Actually, it was more of a shuffle. The dancer rocked backwards and forwards, only occasionally moving her feet like one of the lazed, hazed posy rock artists of the early seventies. She lifted up of her tee-shirt to show her breasts and left it hitched up below her neck. On her heavily made-up face was a blank and expressionless gaze reflecting her boredom at having to go through, once more, her rather uninspired routine. The male customers looked on in a quiet and bland manner, clutching glasses, whilst the female drinkers looked away. The mechanical nature of the dance proceeded without any variation.

"About as erotic as my old ma doing the dishes," said Pete who had by now recovered from his exertion.

One of the group leant forward and said in a cutting and sarcastic fashion:

"Well, if you men didn't need this wet stimulation then us women wouldn't have to provide it."

The speaker was Vicki, a tall, slim, strawberry blonde, bright eyed with Slavonic good looks and a voice straight out of the Marquis de Sade school of charm. The dancer pulled her tee-shirt down and walked off the makeshift stage. Pete looked in amazement.

'Call that a stripper, seen better..."

"Shut up Pete we've got business to discuss," interrupted Victor. The drinkers around the stage clapped half heartedly as the girl moved behind the bar to the room at the back and the barman enthusiastically started to pour drinks.

"Right; Pete, what do you know about Dave?"
"He's in hospital, in casualty"
"And?"
"He's been done-over."
"And?"
"He ain't well."

"And?" Victor was getting angry.

"He's got cuts and bruises."

Before Victor could slam in a further syllable a broad Kentish accent, solid Gravesend, intervened.

"What Victor is getting at Pete, what he is trying to ascertain is what exactly happened." The speaker was Louise. The Queen of computers and electronics, she gently placed her glass of gin and tonic on the table and tapped Pete on the head. "Please use this to tell us what went on."

The drinkers were milling round the bar waiting for the second stripper to appear. On seeing a striking woman dressed in black come from behind the bar the regulars uttered an anticipatory gasp.

"Flipping brilliant it's Catherine!" shouted Pete as he jumped up and beamed across his face whilst Victor looked up from his glass. A beautiful woman had walked onto the stage; Victor's girlfriend had started her dance.

The contrast to the previous stripper could not have been greater. Catherine was a professional. An actress in many soft-core pornographic films she lived by her body and by her brains. She was an artist and a shrewd one at that. Not for her were the images of the exploited woman, downtrodden by scheming men. Not for her was the poor pay and the casting couch. Not for her were the bleatings of feminists in their comfortable jobs. Catherine came from a line of femininity which stretched from Cleopatra through Scarlett O'Hara and onto the modern post 80's woman. She was in control and she demanded and got the best wages.

She stood for a moment on the stage, quite still, a mocking smile playing on her lips. As the opening base notes of T. Rex's 'Get It On' thumped out she caught the rhythm, thrusting her hips from side to side, and with the first crashing drums her arms were outstretched above her head, clawing towards the ceiling. She had started her dance. Clothes were discarded with an elegance that expressed real talent. Whereas the other dancer had avoided eye contact with the men she fixed her eyes on each section of the audience in turn, singling out individuals with a penetrating and laughing stare. Whereas the first dancer had used only a part of the stage she used every inch of it, leaning against the wall to remove one stocking, writhing on the floor to remove the other. Whereas the first stripper had kept arms and legs close to her side she used them to describe wide arches, exploiting every conceivable angle to enhance the erotic. Some of the women turned to look at her dance and she met them eye to eye taunting and teasing them with her sensuality as if to say 'you could never do this for your own man.' The men started to cheer. Victor looked proudly on, but there was still business to discuss.

"Charlie will you tell us what happened, you were there at the hospital and saw Dave, yes? Right, first of all, how is he?"

"He'll have a scar alright but they deliberately didn't go for his eyes or anything, so the hospital says he'll be out tonight after they have patched him up," replied Charlie, "Dave went up to see these blokes up at some pub called The Grapes just off the Old Kent Road to give them a friendly sort of warning about your bid for the video shop and it appears that they are some sort of..."

"Would you concentrate you stupid drip," Vicki interjected grabbing Pete by the collar, "this is important so listen to Charlie and stop gaping at Catherine."

The dancer had taken off her bra. Her breasts were perfect. She started to caress them, accentuating their curves before slowly moving her hands down to her thighs, gently running one finger between her legs. The men started to clap, whistle and cheer and the women started to criticise.

"Mobsters..." continued Charlie "they seem to run the rackets around the Elephant as well as most of Southwark. From what I can gather from Dave they are pretty heavy."

"Sounds obvious to me," cut in Vicki.

"Anyway, they said they are going to expand their business into Kent and in particular they want in on the video side of things. That is why Dave went up to see them because apparently they also want in on the production side of films as well as the supplying. They reckon this county is just going to end up as a stopping place for the continent what with this channel tunnel and all that garbage. They want to get in on the action at the start."

Victor clutched his pint and concentrated on his thoughts, looking rather abstractly towards the stage as if hoping for some sort of inspiration from the dance. Catherine was down to her knickers and the noise in the pub was getting louder as the cheering became wilder.

"They're getting their money's worth today," he said. "Can't hear meself think."

More cheering.

"How much longer she got?"

"That's it, finished," exclaimed Pete who was still on his feet clapping and nodding his head in approval as Catherine left the stage. "You've got a real woman there Victor."

Vicki circled her fist and made a masturbatory gesture,

"Thank heaven for that. Now can we please get on with it... boys," she leered at Pete. "What are we going to do?"

The Lawyer who had been sitting quietly now spoke,

"As I see it there are four options: we can go to the police." His suggestion was met with a series of ridiculing stares. Victor in particular cast a hopeless glance at him. "I thought not. So secondly, we can allow them to take over our video business for a price. We allow a buy out."

"Not bloody well likely!" replied Victor.

"Three, we can sit it out and perhaps lean on some of our customers to stay loyal."

"That's more likely," calculated the boss.

"Or four, we can take them on in a bust-up."

"Yeah," said Charlie, "Good idea. Sort of revenge."

Pete was vigorously rubbing his right eye with the full palm of his hand and was ready to intervene agreeing with this when Vicki's sneering tone cut him off.

"Oh yes. You and whose army? Where's our muscle going to come from? There's only Victor and Charlie who've got any street fighting behind them. Dave's in hospital and won't want another mauling; Pete's a fat, wobbling bit of jelly and the Lawyer is better at running than fighting."

Louise nodded her assent and calmly looking at Victor said,

"That's right. Those blokes are pretty rough up there. I say we use our brains to diversify. Drop the videos and get you started in something else."

Victor didn't like the sound of this. He'd built up his video interests from a very small beginning and was now the leading suppliers of cut-price films in the Medway Towns and was gaining new customers in and around Maidstone, Canterbury, Faversham and Dover. He had bought eight video stores, preferring to rent them out to trusted tenants who would run them for him while he could develop the supply side. Outside of his immediate territory he handled a lot of the dealers, he knew them and the type of customers each one attracted, and he knew all the tricks of cheap importing. He could supply legitimate as well as uncensored films - from Mickey Mouse to the worst of the nasties and he also dealt in quality. The videos he supplied were good and were made to last. This South London mob would flood his market and set back the trade for years and Victor was proud of his trade. He could not let this go. Besides, he could, if the worst came to the worst, call on enough muscle to protect them. There were enough people who owed him a favour to ensure his protection. However, he had never used that amount of violence before and the reliability of it was not quite perfect for a sustained war with this mob.

"OK," he said. "I agree with the four options but I'd like to go for number four. If we let them get away with the videos, what's to stop them hitting Charlie's car trade?"

Vicki and Louise looked worried, Charlie and Pete smiled and the Lawyer frowned.

"However, I don't want to see a face-to-face confrontation. The Class has survived and prospered by sticking together and by using our brains. We've avoided trouble with either the law or with other firms. What we need now is to use our brains to outsmart these Cockney halfwits."

Victor had a way of arguing which commanded respect. He was, after the fourth or fifth pint, quite capable of reasoning and planning to a high degree and he was listened to closely.

"First of all, they must have a stock of videos with which to flood the market. So we find that stock and..."

"Blow it up!" chimed Pete.

"Moron," replied Vicki.

"Dispose of it," continued Victor. "Not by blowing it up, Pete, but by lifting it, all of it. We find the warehouse and clear it out. That is where Vicki, Charlie and myself come in. Then we quite simply lay low and keep trading as usual. They won't know it's us."

The Lawyer thoughtfully asked,

"Fine, but how do we find out where they have their warehouse? It's not going to be listed in Yellow Pages is it? And besides, how do we know they only have one stock? They might import regularly."

"That, Mr. Lawyer is where Catherine comes in. If they are importing or pushing porno-movies she'll find out. There's nothing she don't know about the West End dirty film business. I'll work on my contacts on the nasties side and see if anyone has recently placed an order for a large batch."

Louise broke in on these plans:

"That's perfectly wonderful by me but I have just one little problem, one small thing bothering me."

"What's that?"

"Well just suppose this ain't like a local Southwark mob. Suppose it's bigger. Suppose it's got real muscle and not just five or ten heavies. I mean what do we know about these creeps? Nothing. So just suppose we knock over their warehouse and it ain't like your local small-town suppliers, suppose it's mega bloody huge. What are we letting ourselves in for?"

"A fucking good hiding!" said Vicki.

"A jolly good spanking, sweetie!" burbled Pete giggling in a juvenile style.

"You are a prize pervert Pete."

"Would you two stop bickering. Louise has a point; what I suggest we do is to find out as much as we can first, and if they are just the local mob we break them. If they're bigger we make new plans. Above all we use brains not brawn. You too Pete, start thinking."

Pete looked up at Victor with a happy smile playing on his lips, he liked it when Victor included him in the planning stages of the operation. Vicki buried her head in her hands, hair covering her face as she mumbled something about 'special needs case needs brain cells first.'

"In the meantime I'm going to see if Catherine's dressed and then we're going home. I suggest we meet in a couple of days, like Tuesday, here at opening time. OK?"

The Class agreed and Victor arose from the table that was crowded with empty glasses, a full ashtray and a few empty tonic bottles. He left Vicki, Louise and the Lawyer talking in conspiratorial tones, Charlie getting in another round and Pete concentrating hard on the sporting pages of the Mirror.

"We may be a bunch of misfits but as the Class we're a powerful set-up," he thought to himself, "and we're going to smash those bastards."

Chapter 3

At Rochester Police Station Benjamin began to sift through some papers looking for a list of video suppliers in the South East. He found it and ticked off Victor's name just as his Sergeant came through the door.

"Here's that file on the burglaries in Strood that you wanted." He placed the file on the desk, on top of a pile of other papers. "Any luck with the alchy crook of the year?"

"Not really," replied Benjamin briefly glancing at the progress on this other investigation, " but I think he'll tell us if anything goes on. He seemed to be as much opposed to the whole thing as we are."

"Oh, he would be, dead straight about what he supplies. Only deals in soft porn, sometimes nasties, but not the really heavy stuff."

"An alchy crook with a sense of moral values. Get some coffee would you, Campbell?"

Benjamin sat at his desk and played with his pencil, wondering where to take his investigation from here. Although this was just one of the many cases on his list at the moment it was the one that was causing him the most anxiety. Over the years his work load had steadily increased in tandem with the rising crime level. The days when he had a couple of cases to deal with at any one time were long gone. Increasingly the police were starting to cut corners in solving crimes, they were starting to make assumptions which previously would have been unthinkable and they were starting to make mistakes. This case was complex and it involved children and drugs, a combination which would require more time than he really had to devote to it. Quite a change from the early days when he had come into policing full of ideals of helping the community and upholding law and order. Was it in his imagination or did he once remember a time when the police were universally respected and when a career in the police was regarded as a fine thing? He had joined the force some ten years ago from polytechnic where he had gained an HND which he had then managed to convert into a basic degree. Benjamin was a career policeman and had just come in at a time when the force was getting disillusioned with its university trained officers. He had seen this and was shrewd enough to distance himself from these high-flyers knowing that quite a few of them were heading for a fall. As an officer he had gained the reputation of being efficient without being showy and could get on well with his superiors without being pushy. He was a good team worker but had just the right amount of individuality which marked him out. In bringing him in on this case he knew that something was out of the ordinary and the case was beginning to bother him. It was coming fast on the heels of child abuse cases which were starting to make headlines and were causing concern within Home Office circles. It was also an organised and highly secret operation. A couple of weeks ago he'd thought that he'd cracked the whole ring but just as he thought he'd worked it out the operators had disappeared and nobody knew anything.

Usually in this kind of case the police could interview convicted child molesters who would invariably know something to start their investigations. But on this occasion there was nothing, nothing at all. Even the videos that they had managed to seize at Customs had no genuine destination marked on them, nor did they have the name of the foreign company which made them. The addresses turned out to be false and when they had tried to find out about the company which had sent them for shipment the registers all showed a phoney name. The European connection was worrying. What Victor had sneered at him was becoming true. Criminals had realised the potential of a united Europe almost as quickly as big business had. British policing could not change itself with the speed of the gangsters; it was still attempting to adapt itself to a country of communities and it was still trying to develop an awareness of the problems of differing communities. The kind of training which Benjamin had received was geared more to re-establishing community policing rather than dealing with the rapid, violent skirmishing of international crime. With small time semi-crooks like Victor Manning the police could exist in a symbiotic relationship: they both needed each other to keep out the more dangerous and threatening kind of criminal. But with the current spate of drug seizures at Dover failing to stop the increasing supply of hard drugs Benjamin knew that a new era of crime was opening up. What the country needed, he had concluded, was some kind of British equivalent of the FBI, a national force which could deal with national and international crime. The establishing of the National Criminal Intelligence Service was a breakthrough, at long last there was an organisation which could concentrate on the new, more high powered kind of crime. Doubtless Joe Public would start to scream about the creation of a police state, but what the hell, Joe Public is going to have to realise that the new gangsters were only laughing at their quaint liberalism, were only exploiting their concern for fair play and were using their criticisms of the police to develop their own activities. A national force would have been useful for this case because he believed that this child porn ring was only part of a diversified criminal network which was going to be difficult to break. There appeared to be no beginning and no end in this case. It was starting to bother him.

Chapter 4

Catherine and Victor walked arm-in-arm away from the Lamb and Flag. The brilliant sunshine of the morning had been replaced by a slow and steady drizzle. Catherine was still slightly flushed from her dancing and Victor was flushed from his drinking; both existed in perfect harmony.

Both had brains, both had good looks and both had a set of moral values which placed them apart from 'proper' society. The only major difference between the two lay in their ability to relate to kindred parts of the community. Victor was happiest in the morality of the world of pubs and business dealing whilst Catherine was seen at her best in contrast to the norms of society and to other people. For her, morality was personal and flexible and was designed to further her own interests, Victor's interests and those of the Class. Her looks were classically brunette and her face spoke of a fierce intelligence. Place her next to Vicki and the two of them represented the extremes of female beauty: Vicki the ice-maiden and Catherine the modern Cleopatra.

Victor explained to Catherine about the videos and she agreed with his thinking. She would go into London that afternoon and find out any information she could.

"You know, Vic," she said as they crossed the street and made for their front door, "if there's nothing going on in the city I know of another way to find out about them."

They halted at the door and Victor fumbled for his keys. She touched his arm and said,

"Hang on, lover, I think I'll go straight up to London before the Saturday night binges start. My agent expects me to drop in today anyway. So I'd better see what's happening."

"OK Catherine."

"What I was going to say is that those pubs round the Elephant use loads of Sunday lunchtime strippers."

"Go on, what about it?"

"Well, The Grapes is bound to use some sort of entertainment and those blokes will probably be based there permanent."

The alcohol which had earlier helped in his concentration was now putting him in a more cheerful and playful mood.

"That only happens in gangster movies. Maybe we're dealing with teetotal middle class hoods who hang out in wine bars in Kensington and who like to slum it once in a while."

"Yeah, and maybe Pete's an Oxford graduate who's only pretending to be a special needs case," she replied. "Look, I was going to propose..."

"I accept!" butted in Victor.

"You're pissed again. I was going to say; I propose that I get a job at The Grapes either dancing or serving, and start asking a few questions."

Victor propped himself against the door and with a stupefied look in his eyes replied,

"That's a good idea. Have we any beer in the house?"

Catherine was not angry at Victor's stumbling voice nor his drunken expression. Victor was brilliant when sober and brilliant when drunk. She knew he would spend the afternoon planning. He stumbled through the door and pulled her after him. He slumped up against the wall and held her closely, running his hands over her back and down to her bottom.

"No chance, lover!" giggled Catherine as he tried to unzip her dress. "Five pints of Bishop's Finger in an afternoon session and you suffer from brewer's droop."

"Bloody well don't," said Victor as he gave up on the zip and slipped his hands under her skirt and started to pull down her knickers. Catherine's eyes sparkled as she laughingly dropped to her knees and quickly sprang up, turning round on her heels, freeing herself and sending Victor off-balance. He sat abruptly on the floor and gazed with glazed eyes up at her.

"Oh well, perhaps I do," he mumbled.

She left him sitting on the floor looking abstractedly at her while she made her way in a determined fashion towards the station.

"This is Rochester, this is Rochester. The train now at platform two is the Charing Cross service calling at Strood, Higham, Gravesend, Dartford..."

Catherine boarded the train and sat down. Built over thirty years ago, the rolling stock on this train resembled cattle wagons with seats and the carriages although non-smoking had a permanently dusty atmosphere.

"How people commute in these every day baffles me," thought Catherine.

The train jolted into movement and was soon crossing the Medway bridge. Kent started to speed by the windows. A county once banded together by a combination of beauty and prosperity and existing in an ideology of mild consensus was now starting to fragment. The old style Tory paternalism did not manage to hold back the dynamic of Thatcherism. Small farming and marketing had retreated before the encroaching giant of international trading. The mining industry in the south of the county had been hammered by Thatcherism just as effectively as the village trader; the radicalism of the miners and the conservatism of the individual merchant were being broken by this untamed ideology. Both the traditional Kent industries and the small businesses set up in the early eighties were now collapsing as money and produce shifted across Europe and further with an ease unknown before. Shop after shop in the Medway Towns were closing with the recession and in her own local area she wondered just how long it would be before the number of empty properties in Chatham High Street outnumbered the occupied; shop now whilst shops last was a sick joke which was coming true. Not that change in itself was a bad thing, no community could stand still, it was the nature of the change. The Medway Towns were losing their identity whilst Kent was no longer the garden of England. What really annoyed her was that with the change had come a collapse in quality. People were satisfied by less and came to expect less. Everything existed in the short term. Even in her own business the tacky had replaced the erotic. Ersatz sex had driven the truly classy sexuality underground and shoddy and shabby films had taken over from sensual masterpieces such as Erotic Tales. Granted there were still the Page Three girls with their own brand of well photographed and mildly titillating poses; but how long would that last? The new feminists waving their copies of the Guardian had combined with the Mary Whitehouse brigade to castigate the erotic as being degrading to women, immoral and depraved. This did not so much annoy her as the occasional presence of a politician who would watch her one night and then slam what she did the next day in a council chamber or meeting hall. Catherine would have none of this.

She had seen the hypocrisy of the middle class moralists with their Victorian values. When she had danced in the clubs of the West End she had observed the middle class men hesitantly enter, looking around in case they saw anyone they knew, with breaths coming slightly nervously as they stood by the bar like pubescent boys in a newspaper shop shyly buying a pornographic magazine. They always looked so guilty, always so reluctant to admit that they liked her dancing. They gave the impression of being inadequate, sampling the forbidden before going back to their wives. Most of them, she had concluded would be a lot happier if they got their wives to dance for them.

Nothing had really changed since Victorian times. Catherine had read that prostitution and child pornography were rife during the reign of Queen Victoria and that behind the facade of Imperial upright behaviour and the stiff upper lip there was a fairly raunchy scene going on. There was the respectable West End residential area where these men lead their respectable lives and then there was the East End where they retreated to in order to satisfy their cravings. The two parts of London were kept apart by a society which refused to recognise what was going on. They had also got away with it and like the hypocrites of today they would not hesitate to land the girl in big trouble if their position in society was ever compromised.

This was one of the many reasons why Catherine had joined the Class. Like most working class girls in Kent she had gone to a secondary modern school and watched the vast majority of middle class girls get into grammar schools. She had been intelligent enough to realise quite early on that the grammar school girls were going to make it in life, going onto higher education and getting well paid jobs whilst she and her school mates were going to be consigned to working in Woolworths. From about the age of fourteen she had worked out that there was only three ways a working class girl could make it in life: sport, rock and roll or sex. Well, she wasn't athletic, she'd never make a rock star but she did have looks, a figure and brains. The combination was compelling. She had joined the Class just when it was starting up, using Charlie's contacts in the club world to get work (he had also found her an agent) and being driven to and from assignments by Pete (who before becoming grossly overweight had also been her minder). She had in return pooled a percentage of her earnings for the rest of the Class. That was how it worked; independence within a group, protection within freedom. Who earned the most for the Class nobody could really say. Louise and Dave with their electrical and computer interests (they worked together and had a fiery love-hate relationship) were possibly the most regular; Charlie brought in a fair amount with his motor car ventures; Vicki, who was responsible for investing their profits, was also capable of bringing in huge amounts in a short space of time and then earning nothing for months; and Pete, who was on a wage. Then there was Victor.

She had fallen for him not just for his goods looks or because he was a good lover but because he made no demands on her or her lifestyle. He was someone to go home to and not someone to keep her at home. He was the ideal partner for her.

By now the train had left Kent and was in London; Abbey Wood, Woolwich Arsenal, Blackheath and Lewisham were passed. At London Bridge she got off and looked for a cab to take her to her agent.

At Rochester Police Station Sergeant Campbell handed a file to his boss:

"Thought you might like to take a butchers at this."

Benjamin scanned the document:

"It's only a medical report from the hospital about a bloke being beaten up and needing stitches. What's so important?"

"It's the bloke concerned, he's one of Manning's gang, good on computers. It says he got done over in Southwark but made it back here with a cloth tied round his head to stop the bleeding. Drove himself to casualty and then passed out."

Benjamin placed the file under his arm and led Sergeant Campbell towards the door as if he at last had a purpose and a lead to his investigations.

"Let's go and talk to this Dave Watson character and see what's up. It doesn't sound like a normal punch-up or mugging to me, sounds more like a bit of 'get out of here fast or we'll bust your head open' type of a fight."

"By-the-way," added the Sergeant, "the boss wants to know about those break-ins in Strood. Have we got any thing to go on?"

"Have we got any time to investigate them?" said Benjamin.

"Have we got any extra officers? Have we got any more resources?"

He picked up the file on the Strood burglaries and placed it at the bottom of the pending tray,

"Or are we in fact over worked, over stressed, under paid and over pissed off coppers?" He put on his coat and moved towards the door, "I'll see the boss about them later, much later."

Chapter 5

Below the decks of the cross-channel ferry, a steward was fastening ropes to a car parked in the corner, near to the stern. The air smelt of oil, petrol and the sea. Small pools of water swayed from side to side as the ferry, gently cradled, rocked itself into motion. The owner of the car lounged against the bonnet, idly dusting the windscreen with an expensive handkerchief. The steward finished the last knot and strolled round to the front, admiring the car.

"That's a fine automobile, sir," he said mimicking the actions of the owner by gently rubbing the side window with his sleeve, "I've always had a dream that one day I'd win the pools and be able to buy a Rolls for myself."

The owner chuckled and stood upright,

"Not able to buy one on a seaman's wage, eh?"

"Not likely, sir, it's enough just to keep body and soul alive on."

"Well, here's something to keep body and soul going on a Saturday night," he slipped a folded ten pounds note into the top pocket of the steward. "Now would you keep an eye an the old motor, in case any of the usual lager louts try and mess the paint work."

"I'd say I shall, don't you worry sir. Not that there should be any this early on a Saturday."

The steward started to rattle off a conversation,

"Mind you, you don't know nowadays. Friday night over to Calais, pick up some cheap plonk, get pissed, asleep on a bench, catch the ferry..."

The owner interrupted him,

"Yes, well, quite. If you need me, I'll be up in the bar having a nice large brandy and soda."

The owner moved towards the stairs with a wave of his hand to the steward who continued checking the safety ropes, pleased with his tip.

The ferry began to sail out of the harbour, its lubberly bulk blundering through the stodgy waves until it could get to the open seas and sail with a breeding and grace more suited to a ship belonging to an ancient sea-going nation.

On reaching the top of the stairs the owner stood for a moment on deck watching the ferry leave the harbour before entering the bar and walking towards his two companions.

For a Saturday morning the bar was quite crowded, although many of the passengers appeared to be staring solidly before themselves, concentrating on not feeling seasick. Some started to move outside for the open air, smiling in a guilty fashion as if to say,

"Yes, I'm going to be ill."

A couple of youths lay on sleeping bags on the floor, one clutching a half full bottle of Budweiser, the other moaned slightly and pushed himself up into a sitting position his hands shaking slightly. He opened a crushed, slightly soiled carton and started to crumple the remains of a cold Macdonald's into his mouth.

There were only two groups of people who were drinking and these stood at the long, straight bar. His companions, two well-dressed men, sat on bar stools, one throwing peanuts up and catching them, dolphin fashion in his mouth; the other reading the sports pages of the Mail and chatting to the barman about possible winners in today's races.

At the other end of the bar the second group were congregated. There were six men in their early twenties dressed in an assortment of shorts, tee-shirts and loudly coloured jackets. Sitting round a table were their wives and girl friends in ostentatiously expensive clothes and slightly crumbling hairdos.

After two nights in Paris the style was becoming gaudy and the expense was becoming tired. The owner of the Rolls noticed that the men had drunk more than they could handle, an assortment of continental lagers and spirits forcing each individual to talk louder than his neighbour and in an ever increasingly false sincerity. One of the men leant across the bar and grabbed an unopened bottle of tonic water. Trying to prise the top off, it fell and smashed on the floor, sending an explosion of liquid along the bottom of the bar. The rest of the group cheered, the man swore and stumblingly leant down to pick it up. He grasped a handful of glass in his hand, cutting himself.

"I'll clear that up, sir," said the barman hurrying to the end of the bar. The man clumped the uncut hand on the barman's shoulder and showed him the bleeding hand.

"Don't worry, sir," the barman said starting to wrap a clean cloth over the wound, "we have a first aid centre at the other end of the ferry. They'll clean the blood up with no trouble."

The man jerked his hand away, pulled off the cloth and thrust the hand under the barman's face,

"That blood, is the blood of the workers," he slurred aggressively.

The barman waited for a cheer or a sarcastic comment to come from the men or for a 'come off it' from the women in order to deflate the pompous statement but none came. Instead, one of the men sat the man down on a stool, raised his glass and said,

"To the blood of the workers."

He was answered by a rising chant of,

"Here we go, here we go, here we go."

The barman backed off from the group, smiled and left another clean cloth before returning to the other end of the bar. He'd been in this situation countless times before. Drunken louts would use any kind of language so long as it was associated with confrontation and boisterousness.

Watching this had been the owner of the Rolls; he ignored the drunken group and called a studied cheerful welcome to the other two,

"Ah there you are, you two. I've seen to the motor and now I'll have a brandy."

The accent was clipped public school and one whose cadences stood out in comparison to the drunken scrawl of the cut man. A mimicking and mocking echo came from the other group,

"Oooh, I'll have a brandy."

The cut man rose from his seat, spilling one of the women's drinks and started to chant to the same tune as before,

"OK, yah, OK, yah, OK, yah."

And the rest immediately joined in,

"OK, yah. OK, yah, OK, yah."

"Ignore them, yobs," said the owner.

He took a gulp from his brandy. The taunting continued,

"You fucking hooray wankers," said one of the group, to be followed immediately by the chant:

"Hooray wank, hooray wank, hooray wank."

Many of the passengers started to leave in embarrassment, one elderly man got up to remonstrate with the group but his wife pulled him away. The two youths in the corner pretended to be asleep, whilst the barman picked up the phone for assistance. The cut man began to stagger towards the toilets, swearing loudly, followed by two of his friends.

"Need a piss, need a piss, need a piss," they shouted as the rest of the group joined in.

The door of the toilets closed behind them as the owner of the car said to the other two,

"I'll be back in a minute. Cover me if any one else comes in." He walked with precision towards the door, opening it he accelerated his pace and as he moved towards the gents he quickened to the speed of a predator racing to pounce. He flung open the door and plunged towards the three men at the urinals,

"Right, you yobs," he shouted, "you're going to get a thrashing."

With one movement he grabbed the nearest man and hurled him against the far wall; with another he whipped a small piece of lead piping from his jacket and cracked it across the man's head. The cut man tried to retaliate whilst fumbling with his zip, but the owner of the car stepped back, aimed a kick to his groin and sent him reeling in pain against the urinal. The public school accent rang out,

"Don't bother me again."

He smashed a fist into the belly of the first man and then kicked the legs away of the cut man who fell against the urinal and onto the floor. Standing with one foot on the man's chest he pinned him to the floor and unzipping his trousers he urinated in his face.

"Yobs want a piss, yobs going to get a piss."

The cut man turned his face sideways, closing his eyes, grimacing and cursing as urine splattered in his hair and ears.

"That's better," said the public school accent and he zipped himself up and replaced the lead, "now, if I was you three I'd leave us alone because if you oiks bother us again my two friends will do something to your ladies which could disfigure their faces, acid is so messy you know. And I'll continue to instill good manners into the rest of you."

He left the three men on the floor of the toilet and walked slowly but purposefully back to the bar where there had just gathered the boat's security.

"Everything is OK, now," he said and ushered his two friends out of the bar and onto the deck. They stood leaning over the railings, grinning and chatting. After a few minutes one of the women with the group came out of the bar and strolled up to them.

"Hello," she said smiling at the owner. "you've really gone and done them three over, they're shaking like anything." Her eyes flashed invitingly at the man, "What sort of car did you say you had?"

"I didn't say, but if you need to know it's a Rolls-Royce."

"Can I see it?" she intoned.

"Of course you can, but won't your man in there mind? He might pick another fight."

"He's flat out now, completely out of it and anyway from what I heard you can look after yourself." She sidled up to him and placed an arm around his waist, wriggling against him, "Can I see your car?"

They left the other two still leaning on the railings, grins wider than ever and went down to where the cars were parked. The steward approached them,

"Hello again," he said, "There's still some time to go before we disembark."

"Yes, I know that," replied the owner. "Could you make yourself a bit scarce?"

He slipped another ten pounds into the steward's pocket and moved quickly away.

"And now my pretty, here is my Rolls."

Opening the door he gently pushed her inside and slipped in next to her. He pressed himself against her and ran his hands up her body.

"Comfortable?" he said.

"Very," came the reply. She blew a kiss to him and he sunk his mouth onto hers. Moving his hand back down over her breasts he reached her knee and began to move slowly up the inside of her thigh. She giggled and started to unbutton his shirt, caressing his body as she did so. The violence of the earlier fighting awoke in him a new passion, a new need for conquest and he started to move more forcefully against her, grabbing the top of her thigh and ripping down her tights and knickers:

"Blimey, not so rough," she gasped.

"It's just the way your kind like it, so lie down and take it, scrubber."

He was on top of her now, hands forcing her thighs wide apart, tongue thrusting deeply into her mouth. She gagged for breath and tried to squirm from under him. He had his right arm across her neck and shoulder pinning her to the seat whilst his left hand started to violently masturbate her. The girl started to scream,

"Leave off you bastard, that fucking well hurts."

He ignored her and unzipped his trousers.

"Slut," he breathed as he entered her, penetrating as hard as he could.

"You love it, love it, love it," he stuttered rhythmically with each thrust.

When it was over he pulled himself from her and opened the drinks' cabinet.

"Would you like a drink?" he asked.

The girl pulled her clothes up and turned a tear stained face towards him,

"I thought you were going to kill me. Are you always like that?"

"Not always," he replied, "now do you want a drink or do you want to do it again?"

"I'd like to get back to my friends."

The man shrugged his shoulders, opened the door and let her out. They were nearing Dover and his two friends joined him, one in the driver's seat.

"Right, well that was fun. However, after disembarking it is time for business. So let's get to Southwark as quickly as we can."

Chapter 6

Catherine's agent's office was at Black Friars, in a small backstreet, and as always he greeted her with a huge grin and an extremely pretentious exclamation:

"Lovey, darling, so absolutely frightfully super to see you. I've got an absolutely wonderful role for you in a new film. Bound to get an Oscar for best actress. The role is completely you." He threw his arms around her in a genuinely affectionate embrace.

"OK, Lester" she laughed sceptically in reply, pushing him away and making for the drinks' cabinet, "let's have it. What's it called? Swedish Sex? Young, Hot and Lusty? Naughty Night Nurse? Whenever you put on that voice I know something tacky is coming."

In feigned surprise her agent stammered,

"Absolutely not old girl. This is a classic. It's a modern adaptation of the ancient Greek drama, Oedipus at Colonus. Sophocles wrote the original. Very high brow."

Catherine looked at him in a quizzical manner. Had he at last found her a decent role? Lester continued,

"You play Oedipus' daughter and you are supposed to be quite a tragic character, your father dies and you seek revenge. It'll demand all your previous untapped acting abilities."

Catherine was getting interested.

"What's the film called?"

With a poker face and a measured voice Lester answered,

"Bouncing Boobs in Balham."

In one movement she had swooped up the soda siphon, aimed and emptied half the contents over her laughing agent.

"Oh! Dear, dear, darling, lovey I do love it when you come to see me." Her agent was waving his arms about him as he made his way to his desk.

"You know Lester, if you weren't such a good agent I'd think you'd be the greatest prat alive."

"I know dear heart but then you see you are so much more fun than the other girls. We had a young girl in here the other day, poor thing, only about fifteen and wanted to get in on the act. She was very nervous, kept running her fingers through her hair and flicking her head back just like a young filly. Of course, we had to let her go. I said she ought to go back to school, She said if we didn't take her, she'd find someone else. So awful, but what do you do, lovey?"

"You did the right thing, Lester, and by the way that's what I like about you, you are not a bastard. Quite straight in fact." Catherine meant what she had said. In her business the rip-off was more common than the pay-off.

"Darling, dear heart of course I'm straight. Absolutely tickety boo above the water line, what old girl?"

"You're barmy," joked Catherine.

"Totally round the twist," replied her agent, "and totally lovable with it."

He was by now prancing round the office doing his 'demented Egyptian dance' as he called it. Settling down behind his desk he folded his hands behind his head, leant back and enquired,

"Now, what about this film. It's good pay."

He knew she would agree. Catherine had poured them two large G and T's and had draped herself across a settee. Sipping her drink she said,

"OK, I'll do it because I'm feeling erotic!"

"Wonderful news."

"I'm feeling sensuous!" she panted.

"Excellent disposition to be in," observed Lester.

"I"m feeling carnal!"

"A perfect state of existence. To be completely recommended."

"I'm feeling totally abandoned, wanton and lewd!"

"Katie dear," interrupted Lester leaning towards her, "If you continue in this fashion," he paused before adding, "I'll have to start feeling myself."

He drained his glass in one go and got up to leave.

"Where are you going?" asked Catherine.

"Where are we going you mean."

He had semi picked up Catherine and was half carrying her towards the door.

"Come on star, time to go to the studios, time to make a movie, time for you to strut your unmistakeably brilliant stuff."

"Hang on Lester." Catherine was trying to regain her balance and protest at the same time. "We're not filming today are we? I haven't read the script and besides where's the contract and besides I've got to get home to Victor and besides..."

"Besides, besides, besides, always besides," sang Lester "Oh I do like to be beside the sea side," he warbled on. "Oh I do like to be beside the sea,

"Oh I do like to stroll along the prom, prom, prom,

"And see the pretty girls coming on so strong."

By now he had got her firmly by the waist and was gently pulling her out through the front door.

"I knew you'd be up today, so the contract's at the studio. The film's first rate. The scripted dialogue for today is virtually nonexistent and I've had a phone call from your Victor asking me to tell you that he's had an urgent message to go down to Faversham and won't be back until late. So, lovey, time is money." He had put her down by the car and smiled shyly at her, "Come on, old girl, let's do it, lets make a movie. It's only one scene today, a lesbian fling. Not much dialogue and the crew are waiting."

Catherine looked across at him and said,

"That's what I like about you Lester, you are so smooth."

"Sarcastic bitch."

His car sped off at quite a speed, now was the time to ask him about the videos.

"Lester?"

"What, darling cuddle-bundle?"

"You know Vic's in the video business."

Lester nodded as he went through a red light.

"Well, we think we have a rival. Some bunch of toss-pots have been dumping poor quality tapes on the market. The punters are buying them and Vic thinks we might have trouble fighting this one off. Do you know of any firm that might have got hold of a large amount of imports? Custom-free like?"

He thought for a moment. Although completely flamboyant by nature and slightly foppish he did know when a question had to be taken seriously,

"Light a ciggy for me darling," he said. "I think I might know who your rivals are. There's a firm which is positively busting all customs' regulations to import naughty naughties from the Far East."

She handed him his smoke and he drew on it heavily before continuing,

"And I really think you ought to stay well clear."

"Why?"

"Because lovey, these are not your ordinary crooks. For a start off they are about as big a bunch of brain boxes as you lot are."

This was what Catherine had feared.

"And for a second?" she asked.

"And for the second they took out the Notario family from King's Cross. Completely drove them out, down the Swanee, down the drain; no more Italian prostitution racket, no more Italian naughty naughties. Italian trade gone completely tonto."

"Fuck me," breathed a worried Catherine. "And don't say 'yes please'. This is awful news."

"Anyway Catherine, can't think about it now because you've got a scene to shoot."

They had arrived at the studio. It was a small building, an ex meeting hall or something, so somebody had once said, and had been mainly used for religious purposes. The visitor was surprised by the amount of space inside, like a small theatre in fact, complete with lighting, sound equipment, miles of cable and dressing rooms leading off from the main part of the building. Catherine had shot many films there and had done countless still pictures for the export market. She was pleased to see the standard crowd from the Red Light Film Company. It was nice to see familiar faces. Although quite prepared to strip in a pub or club, film was a far more intimate affair and she didn't quite feel comfortable with new faces around. In a pub you had a degree of anonymity, except of course at the Lamb and Flag, but that didn't mâtter, and you could dominate everything. In a studio the director dictated what was going to happen and you could feel vulnerable after a few takes of the same shot. It was hard to dominate anything laying on your back with your legs wide apart. Lester handed her the script whilst the director, Jim, an old hand at this type of picture, went through the story.

"OK Catherine, this is what happens. You play a bored housewife..." He was interrupted by Catherine:

"Who gets laid about a dozen times, correct?"

"You've seen it before?" Jim exclaimed, taking off his glasses and rubbing the bridge of his nose.

"She's acted it before," retorted Lester.

"Can't your writers come up with anything else except bored housewives, lesbian PT teachers, frustrated nurses or kinky female astronauts?"

"I like it Cathy, we've never done that one before. Kinky astronauts. Sex in the cosmos. Hey, we could adapt Dr. Who. A female Time Lord bonking her way through time and space." By now Jim was addressing the team of camera and lighting men.

"You could have sizzling sexy cybermen," said one.

"And Daleks who said 'ejaculate, ejaculate'," joined in another.

"And the Tardis could be a giant titty," said the third. The crowd of crew men started larking about playing copulating Daleks whilst Catherine went to her dressing room to get ready and to read the small amount of dialogue.

"This take is going to be easy," she thought.

She slipped quickly out of her clothes and looked at herself in the mirror,

"Not bad, lover, not bad," she said sprinkling light make-up powder over her breasts and gently smoothing it in.

She preferred a liberal application of make-up, it softened the effects of the light and gave a more sexy night-time feel to the scene. She brushed her hair and looked critically in the mirror, making sure everything was perfect. After about half an hour she was ready and walked naked into the bright lights of the studio. The scene was set as a bedroom with pale blue walls, a couple of rather stylish mock antique chairs and a large mirror. The camera men looked admiringly at her for a couple of seconds and then carried on with their preparations. On the bed sat the other actress, also naked but less self-assured. Catherine thought she looked nervous and felt that it must be her first time on a set but then she changed her mind as the actress looked at her with eyes that betrayed not fear or hesitation but loathing and hopelessness. She had seen this look before in girls who had been at the rougher end of the trade; from girls who had been exploited, ripped-off and even beaten. It was a look which told of prostitution and desperation, of sadomasochism, of dilapidated and squalid clubs and dealing with mangy and grubby customers.

"This film is not going to be a classic of eroticism" she thought, "not with Miss Suicide over there. She'll have to go."

From the more humanistic observer's viewpoint, hers could be seen as a heartless attitude, showing as it did little pity for the girl who had been trapped in a downward spiral. But Catherine did not believe in the essential goodness of the human character; she believed that there were exploiters and exploited and if the exploited lay down and took it, then that was up to them. She had turned round the situation, changing a normally exploitable position to one where she did the exploiting, raking in the cash by satisfying male lust.

Lester and Jim bounded over to her with Lester being the first to exclaim,

"You look absolutely lovely, lovey."

Jim pushed him to one side with a glance which said 'OK mate, leave off, I'm in charge here' and beckoned Catherine onto the bed. He had wanted to lead her gently by the arm but it was a convention in this sort of film that the director did not touch any of the actresses. He clapped his hands for silence and brought his two hands together under his chin, thinking for a moment before speaking:

"Right then, Cathy this is Jenny; Jenny this is Catherine. I want you Jenny to enter by that door with your dressing gown on, as if you've just had a bath or something. You are both lovers so I want a nice gentle love scene, nothing too torrid..."

"No danger of that," mused Catherine to herself.

"...and you know your dialogue. It's crucial for the plot, Cathy, that you open up with your line about Jenny's character (and don't forget to call her Susan) looking tired..."

"That's an understatement," she observed, glancing at Jenny's badly put on facial make-up.

"...right get to your place Jenny. OK, everyone... take 1... and... action."

Jenny walked through the door, shoulders rounded compressing her breasts, her head was bowed as if already conceding defeat. Catherine got up from the bed and moved towards her, placing both hands on Jenny's shoulders, she leant towards her brushing her forehead against hers. Off the set Jim had removed his glasses and twirled them round muttering to Lester,

"What a professional." Lester nodded in agreement.

"You look tired Susan," said Catherine as she slipped the dressing gown from Jenny's body. Catherine held Jenny tightly and gently kissed her neck, gradually working her way round until she held her from behind. She pressed her body close to her slowly rubbing the inside of her thigh against hers and she began a luxurious fondling of Jenny's breasts.

Suddenly a piercing scream erupted from Jenny as she broke away from Catherine's grasp and stood in agonising defiance with fists clenched, glaring at a man in the corner. Catherine staggered back as Jenny shouted,

"You bastard, you fucking bastard."

She rushed at the man crying hysterically and began to hit and claw at him. She choked on her words as her nails ripped down his cheeks.

"You're fucking killing me you bastard."

The man raised his hands in defence as her nails drew blood. Chaos broke loose in the studio: Jim went to pull the brawling couple apart, Lester flung a robe over Catherine and pulled her to one side, the camera and lighting crew looked shocked. Within a minute it was over. Jenny crouched in a corner with arms folded around her legs sobbing and groaning. The man was standing over her with handkerchief to his face dabbing at the blood. Lester was furiously shouting at Jim,

"You damned wanker, check where you're getting your actresses from next time."

He turned to Catherine and said,

"Get your clothes on Catherine we're going."

"Right," she replied darting towards the dressing room and slamming the door behind her. Jim looked shaken and apologised,

"Sorry Lester."

And calling to Catherine through the door,

"Sorry Cathy, it won't happen again."

Within a couple of minutes Lester and Catherine had left the studio, clutching the contract and the initial payment plus an agreement that Catherine would be able to vet the next actress. Lester took her to the station and put her on the train home.

"All-in-all a rather interesting afternoon lovey," he quipped.

Catherine leant out of the window and gave him a peck on the cheek.

"And a rather profitable one at that!" she added.

Chapter 7

While Catherine had been travelling to London Victor had a message left on his answer phone from one of his newest dealers asking him to come down at once. He had phoned back but there was no reply. On other occasions he would have left this until Monday but Faversham being new territory and needing a period for sobering up, he thought the short excursion might do him good. He strolled down to the station, buying another Cornish pasty on the way. A short way ahead of him he could see Pete plodding along, hands in his huge overcoat, his body rolling nautical fashion from side to side. On calling to him Pete spun round and peered short-sightedly in Victor's direction.

"Hey Pete, it's me, Victor. I thought we'd left you in the pub."

On recognising his boss Pete's face assumed an abstractedly happy smile. He lumbered his huge body towards him.

"I was going to put a bet on before the three o' clock," he explained. "Louise, Vicki and Charlie are still in the pub."

Victor patted him on the back and said,

"Well, put your bet on and then come with me; we're going on an assignment to Faversham."

Pete's smile widened to an outright grin. He liked going on assignments with his boss, and besides he had an aunty in Faversham.

"I've got an aunty in Faversham," he explained. "We can stop by for tea." His voice was a slow and not very intelligible drawl, it dragged out his vowels until they almost stood out on their own.

However, when he was excited or after a few drinks his voice would change, becoming child-like in pitch and breathless in delivery. He went into the bookie's to place his bet whilst Victor waited outside.

Victor was convinced that there was something more behind his inability to speak properly than just backwardness. He thought that Pete may have, sometime in the past, blown his mind away on some pretty strong drugs. His first sight of Pete had been of him painting a wall; or rather of not painting it. For Pete had stood there contemplating a scrawled piece of graffiti, wondering what to do with it. He had stood there for at least fifteen minutes before painting over the offending writing. Victor later learnt that Pete had once needed a new pot of paint and rather than buying it from the shop across the road he had spent £1.50 on a train ticket to buy it in Gillingham where it was 40p cheaper. Pete had lasted just two weeks in that job and Victor, who at that moment was desperate for a driver (he could not drive himself) to move the videos from the docks at Dover had offered him a short term job. That short term gradually became permanent after Pete had proved himself useful as a minder and a messenger. Victor was convinced about Pete's past life when the Class had once talked very briefly about dealing in drugs before unanimously rejecting the idea and Pete had banged his fists on the table with joy at the decision and spent the next thirty seconds rocking backwards and forwards on his chair humming to himself. Victor remembered that he had said something to Pete about being a happy-chappy and Pete had gurgled back,

"Yes I'm a very happy-chappy."

Pete clumped out of the bookie's and put the betting slip in his pocket.

"I've bet on 'Diamond Stud'," he said.

"Good for you," replied Victor not knowing anything about horse racing, "let's catch a train, unless you feel sober enough to drive. How many have you had so far today?"

Pete gazed upwards, squinted at the sun, rested his hands on his protruding beer belly and was about to start to play the bongos on his tummy when Victor put his arm around his shoulder and steered him towards the station.

"Never mind, let's catch a train."

Chapter 8

A Rolls-Royce turned off Walworth Road in South London and cruised slowly down a side street, parking outside a red, white and blue bedecked pub. Three men in tailored suits got out of the car which turned and left them, cutting a swath of wealth through this once prosperous part of London that had, until the last couple of decades burgeoned with new shops, businesses and housing developments. The three men looked like a throwback to the gangster days of the sixties, their suits and confident demeanour out of place with the studied shabbiness of Southwark. Striding through the opened doors of the pub, the leader of the three drew in a long breath through his nostrils as if sniffing the air and in a condescending manner walked towards the bar.

As a pub the Grapes was typical of old London inns. It had once been divided into different bars but around the twenties the partitions had been knocked down and one large bar complete with stage had been created. However, successive owners had maintained the raised section at one end, almost a kind of snug bar where the local dignitaries would drink divorced from the singing and noise from the drinkers below. The local dignitaries would be any thieves, villains or cut throats who had enough muscle to call the shots. The red, white and blue bunting which had been put up at the time of the Royal wedding in '81 was still there, nobody being really bothered to remove it. Inside the walls were decorated with photos of local characters who had used the pub as their regular. It was a novel idea started by the previous owner and which had been carried on. It cemented loyalties and became quite famous as a local rogues' gallery. The photos were not the usual smiling mug shots but a series of portraits which caught the idiosyncrasies of the various drinkers: there was the old sea dog with craggy features; there was the young pool player leaning across the table concentrating on his shot; there was an old lady dressed in near Victorian style; and there was one of the leader of the three men who had just entered. This had angered some of the regulars but he, Nigel Croft-White, had quickly stifled any dissent. Nigel knew that this part of Southwark was becoming less and less threatening, that the real gangsters had moved east, towards Woolwich and out into South Essex. The community could no longer be relied upon to drive away outsiders.

There was a form of apartheid developing in the local pubs with a growing number of bars being associated with one racial group. The Asians were starting to pick pubs for themselves as the tension with the blacks, which had started in other parts of London, was descending on Southwark. Nigel Croft- White had picked an all white pub and played the race card to gain acceptance. He had made sure that the organised racists would not give him any trouble by buying a copy of the BNP paper each month and, for an inflated price.

"Call it a donation for the cause," he had said on each occasion. The three of them reached the bar.

Regular drinkers ignored the group, glancing elsewhere in an obvious avoidance of eye contact. However, one elderly and almost sartorially over dressed lady who had had too much to drink sidled up to them, swaying:

"Buy me a port and lemon deary," she slurred, "look after the people of the manor."

The barman grinned in a nervous fashion and attempted to joke,

"Millie's been down the bookie's today, collected her winnings from yesterday, she's been celebrating, spending all £5.50 of it."

The leader looked slowly from the barman to the old lady. Had there been fewer people in the bar and had he been in a bad mood the woman would have received a string of cutting remarks. Instead he placed five pounds in the barman's hand and said,

"Put that behind the bar for her and make sure that she doesn't bother me again."

The old lady swayed on her feet and took his hand like a servant from centuries ago who had just received a great favour from their master.

"Cor, you're a real gent. I used to know the Richardsons back in the sixties. They were gents but not real gents like you. You talk proper, just like the nobs on the telly."

The leader was becoming bored by her talk and looked across the pub fixing his eyes on a man sitting by the door.

"Hammer old son, you look miffed."

The man rose slowly from his seat and in a grave voice said,

"A word or two boss, trouble."

He raised his eyes to the barman and jerked his head upwards as if giving a command. The barman understood and without a question raised the flap which separated the back of the pub from the main bar area and let the four men through. Tottering to her friends went the old lady, giggling to herself now that she had enough money to keep her in drinks for the next hour or two.

The men entered a small room and slammed the door behind them.

"OK, Hammer, shoot," said Croft-White as he rested his calm eyes upon the man.

"Last night, after you sent me and Marco to start deals with those blokes from the video shop Marco started drinking."

"What's new?"

"Yeah well, you know the opposition? Those geezers from Kent?"

Croft-White shook his head, he had never seen them but he did know that they were the only other people interested in the shop.

"Well, Marco decides to lean on one of them. So he hangs around this pub drinking and waiting for them to arrive."

"You didn't stay with him?"

"Nope. I had other things to do and anyway you know what Mad Marco gets like after a few. Anyway, he gets one of your motors to follow him."

The leader shot up a hand and interrupted him,

"He hasn't gone and banged one of the Mercs?"

"Nope. Anyway, he goes and ends up down in Rochester. Well, Marco parks the motor and follows this bloke into a pub and starts whacking back the hard stuff. He goes and starts mouthing it to this bloke who ain't that pissed."

"Oh, heck. Where is he now?"

"Well, this bloke shoves him out of the pub and slashes him with a cut-throat blade. Made a real mess. Hospital patched him up and he's back here now. However, the filth have got his name and address and they want a description of the bloke what did it."

"I think it would be better at this stage just to give the description and keep our boys in blue happy."

"Yeah, well, he can't bloody remember. Well pissed. So he comes back here and waits for this bloke's mate who was with him. He follows him to the station and starts a fight. Well, he half does this bloke in, but he's a better fighter than Marco and he retaliates. So they both kick the shit out of each other in the end. Don't know what happened to the other bloke but Marco's round my gaff feeling pissed off."

Nigel Croft-White stuffed both hands in his pockets and looked abstractly towards the door.

"Why did I ever employ the idiot," he said, "he's a complete plonker. Look Hammer, go back and make sure he's still OK. You other two come with me. I'm not waiting around any more I want that shop, I want that business. Those two from Kent might think we're a soft touch, so we close the deal quickly and then see what we can see. We go to Dartford, we close the deal, we get the address of the business from Kent and we pay them a visit. I'm not having any more bother over this, I can lean on people far more effectively than mad, pissed, Marco."

An elderly man leaned on the desk at the back of his video store and chatted to his son. Arthur Wilson had bought this business some time ago and had made a steady income but his son John wanted to bring in another company to broaden their outlets and to give them a greater amount of capital to play with. John quite liked this shop. Although small and narrow it had enough shelf space to stock the most popular titles and they were constantly able to bring in just the right amount of new films to keep the customers happy. However, it really was too small and with the increasing number of large video outlets he was worried that they might go under. They had a couple of other shops in similar situations and they were looking for an extension of the idea of either joint ownership or of letting them out for rent. That would enable them to concentrate on developing their East London businesses which were proving to be far more profitable. Of the two offers they had received both John and his father were reluctant to consider the one from the London business and had preferred the one from Victor Manning who had impressed them as a steady operator. Outside the door they saw three men talking with heads close together: Nigel Croft-White and his two right hand men, Sebastian Austen and Dominic Davidson (who had gone over to France with him) were about ready to persuade these owners to sell to them.

"Nothing too heavy you two," said Croft-White, "Seb, you can threaten them but I don't want any violence and Dominic, keep that gun of yours out of sight."

Dominic, who had been slowly pulling a gun from his shoulder holster grinned and slipped it back.

"It isn't loaded," he said.

"Then it's about the first time this year that it hasn't been," replied the leader as he walked through the door.

Seb Austen walked quickly up to the counter and aggressively shouted,

"Right you two little shits what's this I hear from my friend Nigel that you are holding back on us. Either sell us your three shops or we'll burn them to the ground."

Arthur and John staggered back in amazement.

"One moment Seb, I'll deal with this," said Nigel. "Now then, two of my employees came here yesterday, to clinch the deal concerning the ownership of this shop and your other two shops. They proposed that we would have control of your shops and pay you a rent. What is holding up the conclusion of the deal?"

The younger of the two spoke,

"Because we don't really think that a deal with you would be advantageous and anyway who gave you the right to come charging in here using that language." John Wilson was angry, but his father laid a restraining arm on his shoulder.

"Now listen you little oik," Croft-White had forgotten diplomacy in the face of this resistance. "let me repeat what the deal is. We take over your shops and pay you a reasonable rent and in return we offer protection for your north of the river outlets. Where do you have them, in East Ham and Forest Gate?"

"And if we don't?"

"Then what my friend Seb said will come true. We'll burn them and your father will meet with an accident. Nothing serious you know, just something to cripple him for the rest of his miserable days."

The old man looked at his son with eyes which said to the three men 'give in' but which really showed defiance. He hoped his son would fight back.

"And what if we go to the police?" said the son.

"Then quite simply we tell them of your continuing problem with funny substances."

John was shocked by their knowledge and tried to speak.

"Don't bother asking us how we know; we," he paused and

grinned sadistically at him, "have done our homework and I'm sure you wouldn't want to be referred to another clinic. Or perhaps it might be jail this time. And anyway do you really think that the police will believe you against us?"

Croft-White knew that the son felt cornered and he now went for the information that he required.

"I'll tell you what, in return for some information we'll only take two of your stores."

"What's that?"

"There is a firm operating out of Kent who put in the other bid, with a larger organisation than yours. The deal is that you tell us as much as you know about them."

The older man looked at his son who nodded approval before he spoke,

"Look, all that I know is that the boss is called Victor, I don't know his surname, and he owns about five stores throughout Kent and supplies to quite a few others - videos and things like cameras. I know his girl is a soft-porn actress and stripper. Anything more than that I don't know, OK?"

Croft-White stared for a moment at the man and then asked where the shops were.

"The only one I really know is in Faversham. It's called the Video Bug."

"Thank you very much, and now for the rest of the deal. I'm sure we can cooperate."

"We'll think about it," said the son making a move towards the door.

Seb Austen sprang up and imposed himself between the exit and the son, his eyes blazing, a threatening fist clenched.

"You'll do it vermin."

Davidson made a move to unholster his gun but Croft-White glared at him and said,

"Let us know by Wednesday, and do say yes for your own sake."

After the three had left Arthur looked at his son and said in a shaky voice,

"What do we do now?"

"We go down to Kent and see their rivals. Before we open tomorrow we take a trip down to Rochester."

Chapter 9

The journey to Faversham took about thirty minutes during which time Victor had managed to more or less sober himself up and to start thinking about why the dealer had wanted to see him. It couldn't be because of the quality of the films. The last batch of videos were high quality material, straight from the USA: some gangster movies from the fifties (there was still a market for old films), some modern films only just released on the cinema circuit and quite a few nasties. He did not like the nasties. In a similar way to Catherine with her detestation of cheap pornographic films Victor had a dislike of violent films which relied more on gore and graphic details than on any sense of what constituted real violence and the motives behind it. He thought that the classic violent films such as Straw Dogs and the first Dirty Harry movie had been replaced by the explicit but not very forcible films currently doing the rounds. There was no real need for such details he thought; the deaths of Warren Beatty and Fay Dunaway in Bonnie and Clyde were far more effective than madmen running around with chainsaws, slicing people in two and spilling blood like so many rivers of tomato juice. It was similar with horror films. What ever happened to real suspense? Whatever happened to good characterisation in horror films? Indeed what ever happened to classy direction? Ever since the Exorcist gore had taken over and films were getting more and more predictable. One more scene of a character going up a flight of stairs only to be met by deranged zombies or frenzied vampires or maniacal, unhinged, insane lunatics wielding a long sword, an axe or a kitchen knife would send him reaching for his hat and would prompt a swift walk-out to the pub. The Lawyer had just recently been raving about a new horror film based on a story from Stephen King. He said it was a new departure in horror; it wasn't. It was The Exorcist meets the Shining and was not very effectively done. Still, if that's what the punters wanted then that's what the punters were going to get. He'd rather be criticising films for some newspaper or better still push Barry Norman out of his nice little number, but while his lack of contacts, talent and education prevented all three from happening he would quite happily go on supplying them. Not that he hadn't tried to get in on the film business, quite the contrary. He had, like many other youngsters, made many attempts at getting lowly jobs in the industry. However, in common with most of the arts in this country it was controlled by an university educated elite who closed ranks and excluded outsiders just as effectively as the average Medway Town pub. Life, Victor had concluded at a very early age was about fitting in or by- passing and busting through. Therefore, unlike other hopefuls he did not relentlessly pursue his ambition once he realised that the break was not going to come. In that respect he had grown up very quickly, leaving behind his teenage dreams and seizing the opportunity of setting up a video business. And he was good at it, very good. During the past couple of years he had managed to buy five shops and the rent from the manager/tenants paid the mortgage whilst giving him a small profit to start the supplying side; and that side of the business was expanding quite steadily. He knew how to sell and he knew the trends within the industry, anticipating changes in tastes months before they came (it was a standing joke amongst some dealers that Victor had predicted the coming of the turtle mania from the moment the record was released and had very carefully ensured that dealers had their full quota of turtle rubbish to push on the punters before the price of the supplies were hiked up). As the dealers came to realise these particular talents they came to trust him. So why this dealer wanted to see him urgently was a bit of a mystery. Still, there was no harm done, a quick meeting, then a few pints (he knew a pub where they stayed open all day) and then back to Rochester in time for last orders.

They arrived at Faversham and got off the train. Pete looked around him for a taxi.

"We don't need a taxi Pete, it's just a few minutes walk and it's just past the Shepherd Neame brewery."

"Do they brew lager?" asked Pete, as they started to walk away from the station.

His boss looked at him with eyes that said 'if you weren't such a simpleton I'd think you were mental,' before he said,

"For God's sake you nellie. With all the fine pints of good bitter around, why do you have to drink lager? No wonder you get a sweat on from just walking down the road."

Pete had indeed started to perspire mildly. However, he didn't mind, he happily ambled along beside his boss and said,

"Well, it's because it always tastes the same. You can go into any pub and ask for a lager and you know what you're getting. It's the same with McDonalds. You can go anywhere and have the same meal."

"How bloody exciting and how bloody challenging," answered Victor with a tone of voice imitating Vicki at her most sarcastic.

He suddenly stopped and sniffed the air,

"Would you smell those hops."

They had reached the brewery.

"The greatest smell in the world. Let's sit over there for a minute and watch them load the barrels."

Pete, who had started to sweat more heavily lowered himself down on the bench and looked at the brewery workers. They were rolling the barrels down a long plank and onto the lorries. The barrels moved quickly, sometimes slipping and sometimes bumping along, but with a turn of the wrist and a gentle shove the brewery men could control them. Pete started to rock himself backwards and forwards, a sure sign that he was happy. He stared up at the sky and said to Victor,

"Tell me about history, you know, the beer drinker's guide to history."

"You've heard that hundreds of times," replied Victor.

"But I'd like to hear it again watching the brewery men load their barrels."

"OK, here we go," started Victor who had invented this unusual account of history one evening after about seven pints of Greene King's IPA.

"Right, first of all you had the Roman empire and what did they drink?"

"Wine," replied Pete.

"Quite correct. Now that was fine so long as they were only up against other bloody wine drinkers. They could quite happily conquer all the known world. However, in Northern Europe a new sort of alcohol was invented. And what was this called?"

"Beer, beer, lovely beer!" sang Pete to the accompaniment of a regular rhythm patted out on his belly.

"Quite correct again," continued Victor. "These beer drinkers started to gain in strength and intelligence because they were feeding their brain cells with hops and not grapes. They banded themselves together and called themselves barbarians and attacked Rome and destroyed it and all because Romans drank bloody wine. Then for the next five hundred years the beer drinkers fought it out. You had the lager drinkers from Scandinavia who were called Vikings and the bitter drinkers from England. They tried to invade us, but under Alfred the Great who was a known bitter drinker and an eater of fine English cake we drove them away. All through the middle ages this country prospered because we drank bitter. We defeated the bloody French with their bloody ponsey wine at the battle of Agincourt; and when Good Queen Bess was on the throne we defeated the bloody Spanish with their bloody Armada. We only managed to lose America to George Washington because we employed bloody lager drinkers from Germany as mercenaries."

"What's mercenaries?"

"Soldiers of fortune. Men who go and fight for money," explained Victor who by now was warming to his subject. "and you see with places like India they fell extremely easily to us because not only did the Indians not drink wine or lager or bitter, but they didn't drink at all."

"They didn't stand a chance," observed Pete shaking his head in disbelief that an entire nation could go without alcohol.

"So you see Pete, by the time of the middle of the last century this country had the biggest empire the world has ever seen and all because we drank bitter. By the time we get to this century we fought two major wars against the biggest lager drinking nation in the world and we won. The bloody French of course surrendered quite quickly in the second world war because they drink bloody wine."

"You'd have thought they would have learnt after Agincourt wouldn't you." Pete kept shaking his head still in disbelief that another nation could be so stupid.

"Anyway, after the second world war was won by us, the lager drinking nations realised why they had lost and the bloody wine drinking nations realised why they were so weak and they combined together into the EC to try and destroy us and unfortunately they are starting to succeed. This country started going down hill in the sixties and seventies when blokes like you switched to lager. Now that bloody wine is starting to come in we are going to be in big trouble. The EC will eventually ban bitter and force us all to drink their rubbish and then this country will be finished and history will come to an end."

Victor concluded his talk with a flourish of his arms and leant back on the bench. Pete looked happy and thoughtful. This was becoming a real day out for him. He asked Victor,

"After we've seen the video man can we go and see the barges? I like the old barges,"

He was like a child at the gates of a fun fair wanting to see the ghost train.

"The old sailing barges" he continued, "the ones with the sails and things. Like the one my uncle has. Like the ones we saw racing at the Thames match last year."

"Yes, of course we can. There's a pub just opposite where they tie up. We'll have a pint there. However, let's go, business first."

After a couple of minutes they reached the video retailer and walked inside. The shop owner looked at them with a worried expression.

"Nice to see you Mr. Manning, Pete," he said, "Let's go into the office out the back."

Victor sensed something was wrong. The dealer moved with jerky actions, ushering them through a doorway into the back yard where a windowless shed stood. The yard was strewn with half empty bags of concrete and other building materials and an unkept grassy border had overgrown its boundaries. The shed, although a fair size did not look like an office.

"The office," he remarked and led them over some cracked paving stones. They were half pushed inside the dark interior whilst the dealer closed the door behind them. A light was switched on.

On seeing what was inside Victor realised there was going to be trouble. He flung himself at the door and grabbed hold of the handle half opening it when a man crashed his fist into his jaw, sending him reeling against the wall. For a moment there was silence, broken only by the sound of rapidly retreating footsteps as the owner hurried back into the shop. A calm voice spoke out,

"Seb, make sure the owner doesn't do anything silly would you, there's a good chap."

The man who had hit Victor opened the door and followed the owner back into the shop. Pete went to help Victor to his feet who although not seriously hurt was dazed and shaken from the blow. The voice continued,

"We brought you here old man to have a little chat, a little talk about business."

It was a well-educated voice which told of public schools and Henley, of the establishment and power. He was dressed in a smart suit, far more expensive than Victor's own taste. The speaker, Nigel Croft-White was sitting at an old fashioned and battered desk that had become a work top for small carpentry jobs. He was flanked on either side by two well-built men whilst a third sat in a corner with a gun aimed lazily at Victor. The man who had left returned and said,

"There's no problem from the dealer. He's out front wetting himself."

Although less refined the accent still marked the speaker out as being one of the social elite. Pete looked confusedly from each man trying to understand what was going on; business was never discussed like this. The public school accent spoke again,

"Sit down, Manning," it said, indicating a chair in the far corner. Pete moved over to join him.

"Not you fats," it retorted, "stand still."

Two of the men grabbed Pete, one on each arm and pulled him towards the wall. Victor made to rise but a click from the gun halted him. It was aimed more assertively at his head. The voice dominated the proceedings.

"Now listen old boy, we want to make a proposition to you."

Victor was incensed.

"I don't deal under duress," he said. "I don't like being bloody pushed around."

"No, of course you don't, none of us do. However, on this occasion I think a little pushing around might be in order. You see, Manning, we like your business and we'd like to come in on it."

"No chance!" hissed Victor.

"Of course we knew you'd say that, so we worked out two contingency plans. We can continue to flood the market and hopefully drive you out and perhaps put a little bit of pressure on the dealers to trade with us."

"What, like scaring them with guns and violence like that bloke in the shop."

"Well, yes, actually. However, that first plan is rather a long process you see, and we are just a little bit in a hurry. So the second plan is that we deal directly with you and try and convince you that you are in the wrong business. You see we know all about you and your little gang. We know about the frauds on time share and the pornography and the dealing in frightfully risky motor cars. We know about the little electronic business that you have going as well. Oh yes and we certainly know about your delightful girlfriend with her dancing and acting; we have heard that she is quite exquisite. One of these days we will have to come along and see her perform or get hold of a video of her acting. What name does she use?"

Victor did not reply.

"No matter. So what we wanted to suggest to you is that you give up the videos and the electronic side of your operation and let us handle it."

"What's in it for us?" Victor asked knowing full well what the answer was going to be. The owner of the voice got up and walked round the side of the desk and sat an the front of it before replying.

"Well actually, quite a lot. You see we propose that you should be allowed to trade peacefully in your remaining interests safe in the knowledge that you will not be interfered with. We will protect you and your friends from odious little people who might want to hurt you."

Pete who had been quiet up until now interjected,

"But we protect ourselves. That's why we're together. We're the Class."

"Your friend is not very quick is he," said the voice.

Victor spoke, looking at Pete,

"What this lot are trying to tell us is that we are going to pay for protection that we don't need. You know, sort of like in that bloody film we watched last week, Brighton Rock."

The voice clapped its hands.

"What a precise definition of your situation old boy. Although I must say that the cut-throat blades employed by Pinky and his friends are rather old fashioned now, don't you think. Guns and silencers are far more efficient and less personal, somehow less sadistic."

The man with the gun smiled and waved the weapon at Victor whilst the voice continued,

"That sort of violence is so passé nowadays."

"So what?" asked Victor who hadn't understood the foreign word.

"Passé old boy, it's French talk."

"Sounds more like poof's talk to me."

The man with the gun sprang up and thrust it against Victor's throat, pushing his head back against the wall. The atmosphere was destructive, the man's face contorted in repressed rage:

"Any more funny remarks like that and you'll die," he said.

The expression was exaggerated but the threat was real. His eyes raged fury like a maniac who had unleashed all his pent up anger.

"Yes, quite, Manning," said the voice, "Now what do you say about our deal?"

"No dice."

"We protect ourselves," added Pete.

The voice's look changed from arrogant condescension to one of vindictive hatred.

"All right you disgusting little oiks, it's time for some persuasion. Deal with the fat one first."

Victor tried to help Pete but the gun was once more thrust to his neck. The two men who had held Pete now dragged him towards the desk. He was scared now, really scared. His eyes rolled around their sockets and his mouth was open with his tongue curled around his left lip. They pinned him down on the desk, his belly protruding vulnerably. One of the men picked up a plank of wood and brought it crashing down on Pete's stomach. Pete yelled in pain. There came another blow and then a third and a fourth until the screams were replaced by a low moaning and sobbing. They pushed Pete off the table and left him rolling on the floor, dragging himself towards the corner.

"Now it's your turn," said the voice. Victor had not felt fear like this before. His head felt as if there was a pressure inside of it trying to explode, his eyes stared with an intense agony, his mouth went dry and his breaths came in gasps as if it was being forced in and out. The two men who had held Pete now pinned him to the wall while the voice delivered a blow to his stomach. Blow after blow continued: to his head; chest; groin and ribs. With each blow the terror grew in potency, the pressure inside his head racking him in agony. The voice kept pounding him and all the while the pain increased until after several blows to his head the pain was replaced with a kind of numbness and then it began to decrease. One of the men aimed a powerful kick to his groin and Victor slumped to the floor, the men letting him fall. He did not hear what the voice was saying to him, his mind was in a state of insensibility, unable to grasp what was happening around him.   He felt himself slip slowly into unconsciousness, feeling his mind drifting away from him to be replaced by a mist of euphoria. He blacked-out.

Chapter 10

"It's OK, he's coming round."

A female voice gradually penetrated through to Victor's semi-conscious state. Catherine was looking down at him managing to combine a smile with a frown.

"You're all right now Vic, we've got you and Pete back home. You've taken one hell of a beating, but the doctor says that it's mainly bruising, there should be no permanent damage."

Victor was not really aware of what was going on around him, except that he realised that he was in his own bedroom in his own flat and that he ached all over. He tried to focus on the forms around him but only a vague impression presented itself. He tried to raise himself from the bed but that only increased the dizziness. Catherine was forcing something through his mouth, Victor thought it was brandy but there was no kick to it; he thought he had lost his sense of taste.

"It's water, darling. You have to take these pain killers." Tablets were placed in his mouth. "Swallow now."

"I want something to drink," said Victor. "I want some beer."

"Not for a couple of days lover, not until the pain killers and antibiotics have done their work."

Victor was starting to come round, and managing to sit up he asked,

"Where's Pete? He was with me!"

Pete was sitting on the settee with a glass of yellow liquid in his hands. He grinned across the room,

"I'm here. I won the horse race, I won £15 and Shepherd Neame does brew lager, it's called Hurlymann. I'm drinking some."

Victor gazed incredulously at the figure on the settee swigging lager.

"How the bloody hell do you do it? The last thing I remember they were slamming a plank into your stomach."

"I gave in quicker than you did Victor. You should have gone soft and stopped struggling, they'd have left you alone. I couldn't believe how much of a pounding you were taking. I thought you'd never go down. I might be a bit simple but I know how to act in a fight, especially when we are going to lose."

Victor observed Vicki out of the corner of his eye and saw that she was assuming that curious sneering facial expression of hers that she used before launching into a sarcastic comment.

"If you were a top boxer up against Mike Tyson you'd take the money and then take a dive in the first round, wouldn't you?"

Her tone though sarcastic had less of a cutting edge than before as she felt for the trauma that Pete had just gone through. Her face mellowed into a gentle smile.

"Course so, wouldn't you?"

They were all there: the Lawyer standing by the window; Catherine at Victor's bedside; Pete and Vicki on the settee; Charlie leaning up against the door; Louise sitting crossed legged on the floor and Dave sitting on an old fashioned high backed chair in the corner. The chair was Victor's pride, it was antique and was so large that it would have been more accurate to say that Dave was sitting in it rather than on it. Victor called it his throne. The Lawyer had got it for him during an auction. Dave leant back in it and spoke,

"Well, that's three of us that have met this mob. Pete described them to me and they seem as if they could be behind that bastard that did for me."

Dave was slightly older than Victor and had the same smart dress sense. He wore a closely cut beard and had shoulder length hair which was always well combed. He was not really a drinker but enjoyed a glass of wine with a meal and a glass of beer in company. This evening he was sipping on some imported Belgium beer which struck him as being slightly too strong for his tastes. His tastes were fastidious and he was almost finicky in his choice of foods, they sometimes called him the Gourmet. Like his girlfriend, Dave was a near genius with electronics.

By now Victor was aware of what was going on and asked the Lawyer,

"What happened to the owner of the shop? He wasn't willingly selling us out was he?"

"Of course not. The owner is dead scared in case you thought he was part of it. That firm leant heavily on him threatening his daughter if he didn't do what they said. He was the one who got Pete to his feet and then phoned us."

Louise spoke,

"Look, I know this is not going to be a popular thing to say but we have got to start discussing what we do about this firm and"

She hesitated for a moment,

"I think they are too heavy for us. Next time it could be a complete meal that they make of one of us. I mean they might want the whole fucking lot."

The Lawyer cut in,

"Yes, you're right I think they will move in on the entire operation if we let them. No, we have to think about what to do about them."

Vicki sat upright and raised her hand.

"Can I say something?" she asked, fingers outstretched and slightly waving.

"This isn't like bloody school," murmured Victor. "Go on Vicki, what was your point? Could somebody get me a drink?"

Catherine looked sympathetically at him and shook her head.

"As I said earlier, you are not allowed any for a few days, doctor said so. Go on, Vicki, what's your point?"

"I'd like to ask; why are they bothering with us? I mean, we ain't exactly the biggest fucking organisation ever to hit the underworld are we? Besides which we are half legal in our set up. Surely they could hit a more legit target, one wholly criminal. I mean they were taking a pretty big risk with that dealer, suppose he goes to the police?"

It was a question that had been bothering the Lawyer all afternoon, since the first discussion in the pub. He had developed something of a theory which he now shared with the others.

"I have this idea that we are only a stepping stone for this firm, for something bigger. For a start off you say they sounded posh."

"Straight out of public school," affirmed Victor.

"Then they must want something more than we can handle. Unless of course they have that minority public school tendency towards violence. It's not that widespread nowadays but it still exists especially amongst the no hopers. They get dumped you see, washed up on, so they take it out on the smaller kids."

The rest of the Class looked bemused but Victor understood what the Lawyer was getting at and qualified his statement.

"I know what you are getting at, some of those public school reject types are pretty pervie and go in for violence for violence's sake, bullying and all that. However, I don't think this lot are like that."

"They were doing a bloody good impression of it," said Louise and Pete nodded his head and rubbed his belly:

"They were very good at it," he said.

"I don't think so, Pete. They would have tortured us a bit, as well as Dave. No, Lawyer they are out for something else. Why do they operate out of Southwark?"

The Lawyer thought for a minute and, looking abstractedly out of the window, said,

"Two reasons. First, they aren't known in Southwark, which let's face it is easy to get to from Kent and is one of the most broken up areas south of London. It's completely lost its identity; I grew up there remember, there's no community now. The kids are getting smashed on crack and stuff, give 'em their fix and they won't bother you. They'll only mug you if they think you've got money. The kids are going out of their heads. Not all of them, only some but it's enough to wreck the place. So the big blokes move in. It's petty crime meets big crime and these posh bastards are the big crime. They can also slum it there and from what Pete was saying they were dressed pretty smart. Maybe that's their kick: dirt. Some of that sort like a bit of rough. However, the second reason is that Southwark has a history of gangsterism and maybe this firm thought that what remained of the culture could be used for their advantage. It is the last outpost of gangsterism south of the river."

His reasoning made sense. Victor was impressed,

"Now, before my brain manages to shift into gear and provide the answer, why specifically us? What do they really want?"

"I can only guess that we are a stepping stone for something bigger. We will have to find out."

The Class were stumped for an answer. The silence provided a natural break. Pete got up to look for some food in the kitchen and Vicki went to help him. The Lawyer chatted to Victor whilst Dave closed his eyes and stretched out in the chair.

"There is something else that I think I ought to mention. At the hospital these two coppers came to see me and to ask me questions about the beating. They seemed to be more interested than most coppers about the incident and asked if I could describe them. So I did and they went away saying that they'd want to see me in a day or so. They seemed almost enthusiastic about the fight for policemen."

These words brought Vicki back into the room, listening intently. Pete continued preparing his food.

"Was one of them called Benjamin?" asked Victor and Dave nodded his assent.

"Right, everybody I think I'd better explain what might or might not be going on. Pete?" He shouted in the direction of the kitchen. "In here and bring that grub."

Pete wandered back in and Victor quickly explained what Benjamin had told him and had mentioned that he might see a decline in his orders.

"But why would a child sex ring want to break in on our electronic business?" asked Louise, "and anyway why would they go about it in this fucking way. I mean from the little that I've read from the papers it seems as if they keep everything extremely quiet and just in small groups. This seems to be something bigger. I don't think they are behind the beatings."

"I think Louise is right, but how much do we know about child molesters and the way they operate. We are not exactly experts," the Lawyer said, "I think there are quite a few cross currents here which we have to find out about. How, I don't know."

This comment reduced the group to silence to be broken by Catherine,

"I know what we do. We do what I said we should do this afternoon," she smiled at Victor.

"What was that?" he asked trying to remember.

"I get a job dancing at the Grapes and find out as much as I can about them. Vicki can come along and chat one of them up. I'm sure they don't know our faces."

"It's risky."

Vicki supported this idea.

"Not really, they certainly can't know my face and the likelihood of them having seen Catherine dance before or seen her in one of her fucking pervert films is pretty remote."

Catherine went to the phone.

"I'll get Lester to arrange it for tomorrow. It's a bit short notice but he can play it that I'm a visiting artist or some such crap and want to dance in a South London pub."

"That is if they have dancers," said Dave.

"Bound to. If not we'll just stroll along and see if they're there. They might be if they like slumming it and besides they will be feeling pleased with themselves after the beating they gave you two."

The Class agreed. Victor shifted himself in his bed and began to feel better. The tension in the room started to lift as if the group had just found a new weapon with which to destroy their enemy.

Within twenty minutes Lester had phoned back saying that everything had been arranged but warning the Class that this firm was dangerous.

Chapter 11

"Well, that was jolly easy," remarked Dominic Davidson as they drove away from the video store, "A bit of pressure and oiks soon give way. Shall we drop off the happy powder in bongo- bongo district before we go on to the club or afterwards?"

"It's not happy powder that we're carrying and anyway don't be such an idiot," said Croft-White, "do you really think I'm going to take a Rolls through Brixton and start talking to dusky gentlemen? The police might just get suspicious and anyway, I'm not having any of the younger jungle bunnies swiping the wheels off this motor, or nicking the lady on the front. Besides which, before going to the club I want to drop off some of the stuff to an old friend of mine who's achieving great things in the world of travellers."

"What, you mean those hippies camped a few miles away?"

"Precisely. Ecstasy is what they want so ecstasy is what they will get."

Davidson waved two peace-sign fingers in the air and dropped his voice to a low, slow monotone:

"Ohhh, rave on maaaaan."

"Don't knock 'em Dom, these hippies are good customers, my old mate is doing a roaring trade. It's also one more nail in the coffin of law and order. Did you see how the police backed off the other day? They wouldn't kick them off the land, they wouldn't go for a major bust, they're losing control. They're scared, scared of a bunch of love freaks, drop-outs and pill heads. Great."

"What's a mate of yours doing with a bunch of hippies? He could join us?"

"No chance, he actually likes the life, on and off. He's small time really but there's some big rave coming up and he wants a few extra pills. Approx. £500 worth."

Seb Austen, who was driving commented,

"It's not been a bad day so far, has it. Nigel cracks a few oiks on the ferry; we clinch the deal on the video stores."

"I hope we do," said Croft-White.

"Then we severely harm the Rochester dealer and his fat friend, who by the way ponged to high heaven, and now we go off to the country to sell some jumping beans to some throwbacks from the late sixties. God, I love this job. Drugs, violence, all we need now is some sex. What's the chance with one of the hippy chicks?"

"I don't know and anyway Seb from what I hear you prefer the violence to the sex."

"No I don't," he replied before adding, "well, not often. But you must admit you can't beat a good ruck followed by a good bonk."

The other two laughed in agreement as the car left Faversham and headed out towards the countryside.

Davidson and Austen were Croft-White's closest friends and employees. The rest of his mob he ruled with a mixture of fear, money and the chance to live the good life. And their way of life had become very good, rising from a chance opening a few years ago to becoming near major figures in the underworld. They were not as yet in the big league but it was coming and it was coming quite fast. They had followed their predecessors and created a culture based on fear and violence. It was the way all successful rulers had operated; fear was respect. But the violence was becoming more random and less well planned and that was taking the enjoyment out of it. There was no point in doing over a minor figure who just happened to get in their way. Violence had to be anticipated, worked for and a tension created. He, like Davidson and Austen got a buzz from violence just so long as the victim was not passive. There wasn't any real point in beating up a victim if there were three of you and just one of him, there wasn't any real danger or any real threat, there was no element of conquest involved. He had read some time ago a book about ancient battles and had immediately admired the warriors of old who used to throw themselves at the enemy. When the two armies had assembled and faced each other a group of about a dozen warriors would come out from one of the armies, stand in front and face the enemy and work themselves up into a frenzy. It was called going berserk and when they had got themselves up into a frenzy they'd charge into the enemy. Often the very sight of these dirty dozens would send an enemy running scared.

Croft-White liked that. He thought that it was the British way of fighting; going against an enemy with the odds stacked against you.

So the incident with Victor Manning and his fat friend didn't really satisfy him, but it had to be done for the good of the business. He looked forward though to a revival of gang violence because there they would prosper. With a network already in place and some of their best heavies having been blooded in football matches on the continent he felt that they were well placed to dominate the local area and, just as importantly to deal with any European development that was bound to happen. Europe was going to be good for Croft-White; with the restriction of goods being lifted and with the free flowing personnel he should be able to set up organisations right across the continent. It would also mean that a continental style of crime culture would come across and this combined with the increasing American influence meant that London would become quite a violent place. Already guns were appearing on the streets and London itself was starting to resemble New York with its segregation of the various racial groups. That suited Croft-White, the closer London came to New York the better he liked it. He even had a couple of local politicians in his packet. Not as much as the villains of the sixties had, but then the local Labour Party was run by a right wing Mafia who were very open to bribes and favours. But now a new puritanical and idealist type was starting to take over which effectively cut the gangsters out. That was unfortunate but not threatening to them. Croft-White had a keen sense of political power, it was one of the few benefits which a public school education had given him.

While he had been at school he had gained a reputation for being able to get hold of almost anything the other pupils wanted, for a price. He was also something of a card player. One of his teachers had said that he would end up a teenage tycoon. He hadn't been far wrong. Thrown out of his first school for using drugs he had decided that a normal, mundane existence was not for him. Not that he had resented his schooling, far from it. It had given him a certain level of intelligence which was now useful and it had given him self confidence. It was just the life style of the standard middle class existence which alienated him. School, university, a career in one of the good professions, that meant nothing to him. He wanted glamour, excitement and above all he wanted recognition. Calculating each move in a ruthless fashion, he had no qualms about the consequences of his actions. If he wanted something then he made sure that he got it. It was impossible for him to distinguish between the varying types of crime or attempt any real moral evaluation; the world was there for his disposal to use as he thought fit. Should the police ever catch up on his activities then he had no doubt that he would die first before accepting imprisonment.

Austen and Davidson had also gone to public school but it was in a squat in Camden that they had first met him. The fact that the house was designated for a local did not seem to really bother Nigel. The fact that they had taken a home away from a couple with a disabled child did not alter his feelings. He wanted to stay there and he did his best to ensure that they would remain there. It was this determination which had inspired them plus an almost complete disregard for personal safety. They had been taught at school that certain values should be upheld and that there existed a form of personal honour and correct conduct. Croft-White had arrived at the squat and after a time had befriended Dominic and Seb, showing them that loyalty to one's friends was far more important than loyalty to society. And he had stood by them. When the local heavies arrived to throw them out Croft- White had been the last to leave, fighting and kicking as he was thrown down the stairs. When a couple of the local people started to hit Dominic, Nigel had gone for them and managed to bring two of them to the ground. He was not going to be pushed around and besides he wanted other people to see that he was not afraid. Since that moment Seb and Dominic had followed him through his different ventures with a growing belief that they were invincible.

As such he was really two people: the charming and intelligent public school graduate and the violent and narcissistic thug. Not that he was a split personality; no, the charming and the violent could exist together quite happily. He was what doctors might call a sociopath, a person who had no remorse for his actions, and as such was indistinguishable from many politicians, journalists or city businessmen. He had once thought of going into the city and earning a steady income, but the lack of real danger and excitement deterred him. During the early eighties when he was just turning twenty he had had a brilliant idea for a night club and had sold it to one of the new club owners in London. The club took off and cashed in on the new romantics burst of '81 to '83. This had given him the initial capital to explore other areas and he had slowly but progressively abandoned any attempt to be legitimate and had gone almost entirely criminal. Only one activity remained legal and that was his club in

North London. Small and exclusive, the Club was his front. They would go there tonight, but first they would approach the Travellers' camp.

The camp was sprawled across a large, divided field with the Travellers' caravans and tents laid out like draughtsmen in the middle of a game of draughts. At the entrance stood a painfully thin youth, gaunt of face with large ears extending above the base of a rolled up woolly hat. With bulging eyes he glared wildly at the new comers with a stare resembling the classic portrayal of Nosferatu in the early and most sinister 1920's version of the Prince of the Undead. At the other end of the field stood a huge wicker man, symbol of the pantheistic religions of old, a solitary figure, statuesque and ready to be burned in sacrifice. Around this giant a dozen unkempt children played simple games with makeshift toys. A staked and restrained Rottweiler tugged and wrenched at a too frail piece of rope in an attempt to join in. In the middle of the field stood the caravans and tents encased in an odour of camp fires, cooking and unwashed bodies. The pungency of the smell was matched only by the pungency of the music. Thumping base notes joined with sampled extracts of past songs to create a modern Dionysian music.

The people could be judged as to their dedication to this style of life by their clothes which, as with so many past fashions came to represent a kind of grade or rank within this disorganised group. Continuing from the middle eighties designer ripped jeans came the inversion of normal dress rules; the scruffier the individual the more committed, and, probably the more middle class.

As the Rolls-Royce approached the camp Croft-White slowed to a crawl and waved to the youth at the entrance who glared back, rolled his eyes several times and pulled an involuntary distorted face like an insecure and nervous adolescent.

Austen leaned forward in his seat and glared back.

"Heck Nigel, he's just pulled a face on you," he said, "stop the car and I'll sort him out."

"Don't bother, he's just screwed up, a bit of a crack head. He went to the right school though."

Davidson paid no attention to this conversation, he was staring to his left,

"Blimey look at that chick with the tits, flipping enormous. Girl like that ought to wear a bra or a tee-shirt or something. They're obscene."

"I bet she could wear them for ear muffs during winter," joined in Austen, "but look over there at that guy with his shirt off, talk about tits. He must have a chest measurement of about 46. Guys like that should not be allowed to walk topless, now that is extremely obscene."

"Disgusting," added Nigel, "But that's what happens at places like this. Anything goes, no holds barred."

By now the travellers who had seen the Rolls were stopping what they were doing and were looking curiously at the car, not in a threatening manner but as if to say 'what the hell are you lot doing in a place like this.' Austen felt slightly uneasy.

"Well, I'm ready for a fight if they start anything. But I don't know about the Rolls Nigel, a bit risky for the paint work."

"No danger, this motor is safer here than on many a street in London, a lot of these drop-outs come from a background of wealth. Reminds them of their past, so to speak. Anyway, we represent the mainstream life style, they probably feel sorry for us."

"Cor, I hope that feeling sorry for us leads to some charity because I'd love to fuck a hippy chick," said Davidson.

"You might get a chance later. My old school chum will put in a word for you," said Croft-White as they pulled up against an extremely dilapidated caravan, "there he is, pissing up against that tree. Oh! Brownslow!"

The hailed man turned round still urinating. He looked short-sightedly towards the car and then grinned, zipping himself up he called back,

"Croft-White! Still sound are we?"

"Extremely. Now if you've finished emptying Mr. Thomas against that poor maligned tree could we talk some business?"

"Surely. Sound business." They shook hands and Seb and Dominic were quickly introduced.

As they walked towards a smarter caravan Austen continued to eye the topless woman, who cast a glance back at him.

"If I don't get my dick in between those tits and give it a good rub I'm going to have to bash the bishop silly tonight."

"Go on then Casanova," said Croft-White, "pull her. That OK,

Browny? No problems with it?"

"Croft-White, this is a free community and she's a free spirit."
Brownslow spoke with an authoritative voice and a dismissive gesture
with his hand. "Fuck away old boy, enjoy what nature gave you."

Austen needed no further encouragement and followed the girl
who was leading him towards a small tent. The three men looked
after him, smirked at the leisurely chase and then entered the caravan.
Inside, a josstick burned quietly in one corner, a heavy crimson
lampshade dulled the light to an orange glow and a miniature light
show cast shadows against the walls. In another corner, draped across
three floor cushions lay a naked woman of about 25. Head thrown
back against the drop of the cushions, she had passed out and a joint
still mildly burned between her fingers. Brownslow settled himself in
the middle, paying no attention to the nude. Croft-White did likewise
and turned his back on her, but Davidson could not take his eyes off
her. It wasn't so much that she was beautiful, because she was in fact
quite plain, nor was it her figure, which was somewhat on the small
side; it was just the fact that she was so unconcerned with their
presence which enthralled Davidson. Austen took a joint from a box
and lit up.

"Want one?"

"No thanks," replied Nigel.

"Dom?" he enquired to no response.

"Oh dear," he sighed, "your friend is obviously not used to our
little ways here, is he Crofty? Not very sound."

The two men looked at Davidson who was still staring at the
woman.

"OK, old thing have a go. You play with her whilst Crofty and
me go outside."

Davidson cast a quick glance at his boss who nodded in the
affirmative before getting up and leaving the caravan. Brownslow
followed whilst Davidson crawled towards the prostrate figure.

"Hey babe," he breathed.

There was no reply. He took the smouldering joint from her
fingers, leant over and kissed her. There was a faint raising of her
eye lids as she looked blankly at him. He kissed her again but this
time more forcefully. The woman rose slightly to her elbows, lolling
her head forward trying to concentrate on him, but then she fell back
to her original position with her head back and her mouth open.

Davidson gritted his teeth and hissed,

"Fucking hell, she's out. Never mind."

He took off his shirt and started to rub his chest against hers, slowly at first but then with more pressure and quicker. She still did not move, completely unconscious. Needing more Davidson undid his zip and crawled further up her body:

"Here it comes babe, and your mouth is all ready and opened for it."

He slid his erection into her mouth and groaned. Quickly reacting to his passion he turned round and placed his head over her tummy, lowered his penis into her mouth again, pulled her legs apart and started to rapidly flick his tongue across her vagina. A faint choking sound came from the woman and Davidson pulled himself away.

"I ain't having her close her teeth on my dick," he thought. "God, I'm going to spank her, hippy chick."

With one hand he turned her over onto her side and then rolled her onto her stomach. As he did this he started to grab her buttocks with his other hand, kneading the flesh as if it were a lump of dough. Having finished moving her into position he started to masturbate himself whilst at the same time he started slowly and rhythmically to slap her. Not too hard at first but then as his own gasps came quicker and as he started to masturbate himself faster and faster so he started to hit her harder and harder. He stared down at the flesh every time it shivered as he hit it, he became unaware of how hard he was hitting her, but still he hit and hit and hit.

A crash came through the door as Brownslow rushed in followed by Croft-White. They grabbed Davidson just as he was about to ejaculate. He pulled himself free and at the moment of ejaculation buried his penis into her hair.

"You fucking maniac," shouted Brownslow. "I said you could play with her not fucking well kill her. Croft-White you've got a flipping lunatic on your staff."

Nigel was unconcerned but looked knowingly at Dominic.

"I know, but he's a fucking good fighter. A bit pervie is our Dominic," he said.

Davidson wiped the last of his semen in the woman's hair, zipped himself up, put on his shirt and hissed,

"Fucking good."

Brownslow was unimpressed and looked at the growing marks on the woman's buttocks.

"It's not really on, Crofty old boy."

"What, not even for an old school chum? I'm sure you can explain that one away. Anyway, Browny, can we talk business?"

"Yes, of course. Shall we go outside again?"

"Nope, here will be fine. Gives Dominic a chance to look at his handiwork."

Davidson leant back against one of the walls and laid his legs across the woman's buttocks.

"Nice, soft leg rests," he commented.

Brownslow cast an unnerving glance at Davidson and muttered to himself,

"It's really not on."

He turned to Croft-White and said,

"OK, let's talk business. Some sound stuff is needed down here at the moment and the payment will be just right. However, we might have to hold something on account. The giros are not due until next week."

"What giros?" asked Dominic.

"From the grateful tax payers, old thing. We are keeping off the job market and thus allowing other more mainstream people to get a job."

"Nice life if you can get it," he said bouncing one leg up and down on the woman's behind.

Brownslow was getting irritated.

"Nigel, do you think you might get him to leave her alone. She didn't consent to that sort of thing you know."

"Is that important?"

"Too right it is."

There was anger in his tone which both Davidson and Croft-White sensed. Davidson continued the bouncing.

"Bouncy, bouncy, bouncy," he sang.

Nigel moved across and slowly picked up his legs and rested them on a cushion.

"Enough bouncy for now Dom," he said, "we are, so to speak guests here."

Davidson got up and left.

"I'm going to see what Seb is up to with thunder tits," he said

"Hell fire, Crofty you've got a mad man working for you."

"As I said earlier, bloody good fighter. Now, Browny old thing, when will the payment come? Next week at the latest."

"Absolutely. There is no problem. Usual rates?"

"Yes, usual rates. Let's go to the Roller."

As they moved outside Nigel asked Brownslow one last question,

"If we need any of your lot for a bit of heavy work will you be able to provide? Free coke of course."

"Absolutely. See that guy over there," he pointed to the tall gaunt youth, "Part of our defence force. Bloody amazing fighter, goes mad, screams and everything before going for the opposition. Scares them half to death."

"Good. Right, here you are."

Croft-White undid the boot of the car and picked up a cellophane wrapped bundle of pills. He tossed it to Brownslow, who caught it and threw it up in the air in a 'how's that' catch. He handed over a rolled wad of bank notes.

"From the grateful tax payer," he said.

Austen and Davidson came out of a caravan, Austen still putting on his shirt and grinning widely.

"Fucking amazing," he said.

"Well I hope you left her in a better state than your mate here did", said Brownslow.

Croft-White and Austen got into the car and Davidson climbed into the driver's seat giving Brownslow a parting stare in the eyes. The Rolls moved off and Brownslow stood watching them.

"It really wasn't on," he said.

Nigel didn't comment on Dominic's violence that afternoon, he didn't really care what his employees did so long as they did their job for him. He also knew both Dominic's and Seb's pasts. Both Dominic and Seb had been spoilt as children; Dominic by parents who were always away and who sent money as a substitute for affection, and Seb, whose parents had tried every single educational option they possible could before they realised that their son was not going to make it academically. So they bought him expensive clothes hoping that it would spur him on to get a good job. It hadn't. He had left home and gone to London to live in a squat. He had started off by being extremely left wing and 'alternative' but he soon dropped the pose when he met some real left wing people and decided that he didn't like their attitudes, their politics, or their committed life style. So he had followed Nigel Croft-White and had slowly acquired far more possessions than he ever could have with a mainstream job. Seb handled the drugs side of the operation, and was particularly good at selling to the West Indians, while Dominic hired the heavies and ensured that their various customers paid up on time. Seb had been drawn to violence at an early age. He had been part of a hunt meeting when he was fifteen and had ridden to hounds. They had chased a fox across several fields and Seb, although not a great rider had been almost mesmerised by the exhilaration of the hunt. He had been up with the hounds, fording streams with them and crashing over the small hedges. The rhythmical plunging of the horse's haunches and the pounding of the hooves had made him breathless, gasping for air, feeling his throat tighten. His eyes had stared as wildly as the horse's and saliva had dribbled uncontrollably from his mouth. When they had trapped the fox he had watched the hounds leap on the animal and start to tear it to pieces. His horse had reared up in a sudden stop, almost throwing him to the ground, but he had stayed, fascinated by the slaughter. A few months later he had been involved in a fight and had slashed the opponent across the face with a knife. The knife cut deep and his enemy had raised both his hands to protect himself but as the blood started to flow Seb had felt a delight in the thought of the vulnerability of his rival and had slashed again, cutting right across his hands, splitting them deeply. The man had slumped to the floor and Seb had watched as a pool of blood had formed, slowly spreading, inching its way along the floor, breaking into little rivulets and spreading itself out like the strands of a web. Since then Seb had decided that he liked violence. Dominic had no initiation into violence, he just thought it was fun.

"So Seb you old dog," said Nigel, "what did you get up to with miss floppy tits?"

"S&M," hissed Seb. "She's well into it."

"So you got consent did you. More then Dominic did."

"Well, not exactly consent, at least not for all of it. But you know women, they say 'no' and they mean 'yes'."

"Oh well, they're only drug heads," said Nigel.

"Yeah, good customers," replied Dominic.

Having left the cocaine at the warehouse they drove up to their club. The doorman greeted them cheerfully and told them that their guests had already arrived. Croft-White climbed down the narrow winding stairs to the cellar bar. This was the private part of the club for special invitees only. Hewed out of the ground by the original owners of the club it had been slightly expanded by Croft-White and now contained a small bar. The cellar bar had that slightly damp or musky smell which seemed to go with subterranean rooms and when filled with smoke it could quite easily pass for a secret speak easy from the twenties. That was exactly the atmosphere that Croft-White wanted to create. It was a pity that fire regulations prevented him from putting more tables in but as this was the legitimate face of his business he had decided to play this one exactly by the books. There were about thirty tables, half of them taken, and the conversations flowed in a good humoured fashion. Special club members enjoyed the exclusivity of the cellar bar where deals could be struck or girlfriends entertained by the regular blues trio, or where some serious drinking could go on. Most of the regulars knew of Croft-White's other activities and in turn the clientele had themselves become a mixture of the minor criminal or those that needed to acquire goods and services that were not quite legal.

As his two guests saw them one of them let out a juvenile scream of recognition as the other stood up and waved his arms in an arch.

"Crofty, how wonderful to see you again," he shouted in that typically loud public school accent, "and here's Seb and Dominic, went to the wrong school but never mind. Let me buy the drinks."

"Jolly good of you," said Croft-White whose accent had shifted up a gear.

He now started to talk in a real, old fashioned, public school diction.

"Now, I've managed to get everything in order and things are progressing quite nicely," he proceeded "We shall pick up the tapes from Dover tomorrow morning, store them in our London warehouse and then shift them that night to the various outlets. After that, by Friday, we should have about seven shops in Surrey and Kent for distribution."

His style of talking was now quite distinct. It was not just the upper class accent which he used on most occasions and which was often the subject of mimicry by impersonators. This was the genuine public school accent which was nearly impossible to mimic. Historically, it had been a manufactured style of speech, without roots in any county. It had been created as a badge of identification so that no matter where an English public school educated person went he could be recognised. It had been essential during the days of the Empire when the public schools had trained the administrators of Empire and particularly useful in the running of the Raj. The colour of a man's skin might show he was of North European origin and his passport might show that he was British but the only thing which could tell whether he was 'a sound chap' was his voice. It had often amused Croft-White that some blacks from Africa or the West Indies whose first introduction to English had been through a public school educated missionary would talk in the same style as he did. He had once heard an hospital orderly in a London clinic talk impeccably in a public school accent. Many people had tried to imitate it in the past but none could sustain it over a conversation.

The drinks arrived and the group started to chat in a joky manner and as always when people from a similar school, college or club get together the initial talk was one of nostalgia.

"Are you still striking controversial poses Crofty? Gosh, do you remember when you walked goose step down Lewisham High Street giving the Seig Heil salute? That was taking a risk."

"And you were dressed in black tie and dinner jacket."

"Those days are slightly over. Anyway it wasn't as bad as you getting drunk, throwing up over the housemaster's study and then falling out of the second floor window."

They laughed uproariously in an exaggerated fashion, thumping their fists on the table and talking even louder. They felt happiest when they were the centre of attraction and the small crowd in the bar turned to look at them for a couple of moments. The conversation continued for some time until they turned to business. Croft-White spoke first.

"Now you chaps know that I'm only doing this out of loyalty to old school chums don't you? It is just a little bit risky and whilst I don't mind risk, in fact I love it, I'd rather go down for something just a little bit more respectable, if you get my meaning. I mean to say, I've got nothing against child pornography, as you know I have some pictures from the Victorian era, but the law does not exactly give a light sentence for distributing this sort of thing."

"Don't worry old boy, the police will never be able to trace it to you, not with the system we worked out. It's perfect, especially with 1993 about to arrive. All over Europe we'll go. The police won't be able to cope. It'll be capitalism gone rampant, we'll supply absolutely the entire continent within a few years, and what with the commies getting stuffed in Eastern Europe and the ending of all those restrictions we shall be able to open up the market for this sort of thing right across the board."

"That's the main reason I'm doing it, to get into Eastern Europe. Those Slavs and Polacks won't know what's hit them when we start supplying. We'll be able to sell them absolutely anything with a Western tag on it. And then we'll shift the drugs operation from this country over there and get them smashed out of their skulls. The Commies couldn't stop the opium of the people so now nobody is going to be able to stop the real thing."

This reference was lost on Seb and Dominic but his two friends raised their glasses.

"To Karl Marx and the real opium."

"There is something else which we ought to tell you about, who will be buying these videos."

"Go on," said Croft-White.

"The list contains some pretty important people. No MP's although there is one MEP, a few senior court officials and some influential business chaps. They are all working through the old boy network, but it's crucial that this list is split up. We've allocated each one to a different supplier so that if one goes down he won't take the rest."

Nigel thought for a moment,

"I'm interested in the MEP. I want to get in on this Europe thing. There are some ultra right wing people in the European Parliament and this sort of product seems to appeal more to people on the right than the left. Any chance of a meeting?"

"Afraid not old thing, this is to be kept absolutely quiet. However, I can put you in touch with the French right, they have a fair number of crooks and villains amongst them."

"OK thanks. Now, how about a few more drinks?"

Chapter 12

The next day Catherine sat on the steps outside her front door and waited for Charlie to pick her up. She knew he'd be late because he would have to call on Vicki first and getting that lady up at ten in the morning was a difficult task. Vicki was essentially a night creature and had not lost the youthful ability of being able to party all night, have a couple of hours sleep and then go to work the next day. Catherine, although the same age (they were both 22) had found that an all night stint would leave her worn out and feeling unpleasant the next morning. That was one of the main reasons why she had left club-land; most of the work did not start until after midnight and would often go on until five or six the next morning.

She had always found the West End a depressing place to be at first light. The neon signs no longer created an image of magic and glamour but highlighted a landscape that was littered with debris from the night's excesses and accentuated the dowdy and unimaginative skyline. The star light from the previous night had grown cold and Catherine always thought that London at 6.00am was the nearest a city was ever going to come to having a hangover. The last straw for her had arrived one morning when, tired and feeling somewhat cheapened by a rather shabby club, she had walked towards the station to be greeted by a cheerful 'good morning' from an employee of McDonald's cleaning the front paving of the fast food restaurant. It was the puritanical cheerfulness combined with the thought that the only place starting to function at this time in the morning was a bastion of mediocrity which finally convinced her to quit the West End. McDonald's she had concluded was like one of those evangelical religions, always presenting a smiling face to the world, always just perfect and safe and always pumping out the same message. The McDonald's culture was making the city safe and Catherine did not like safe cities. Those who told of danger in cities and who spoke of the risk of violence did not fully understand what a city was. London had always been a dangerous place to be, that was part of its charm and its excitement. It was a place where creativity could thrive amidst a culture based on risk. The McDonald's culture and the culture of the puritans would destroy London by destroying the danger. Little was new in London, everything was becoming a cover version of something else; like all those countless cover versions of past great records, London was a cheap recreation of a London long gone. She had decided to get out.

So now she had come to like the Medway Towns for being just that little bit different. There were really two quite distinct ways of life living side by side. In Rochester, just down the high street was the world of the tourist and the Castle: of exotic goods in quaint shops and of restaurants each one of which desperately tried to 'out-Dickens' every other shop or restaurant in the street. Why the town had plumped for Dickens seemed a bit of a puzzle to Catherine, he hadn't been born here after all. Lived there yes, but it was pushing it a bit. Catherine had found this part of Rochester hilarious.

"I mean," she had often said to Victor, "fancy calling a restaurant The Oliver Twist or a wedding dress shop The Miss Haversham. Someone must either be pretty stupid or have a wacky sense of fun."

She had wondered whether any new school in the area might call itself The Thomas Gradgrind School or The Mr. McChokemchild College. She put nothing past the council since it had once spent a few thousand pounds on spraying the high street with false snow during a Dickens' festival.

Yet just a couple of hundred yards away from this showy frontispiece was the Troy Town community. Apart from the pubs which remained insular the area presented a far more genuine picture of Medway town life. It remained a small haven of spontaneity against the contrived life of the Castle end. Occasionally the spontaneity took an ugly turn; there had been three stabbings in the past couple of months outside the pubs on the Chatham High Street, bringing to the surface a potential for violence which had always just lain hidden. Victor had once told Catherine that he thought a writer and photographer could capture the two sides of Rochester and present them in a documentary. Catherine thought that the producers of the documentary would get it wrong. They would portray the City as being one of light and colour and activity whilst the working class area would be presented as drab and dark. It would be a false impression. It would be like the presentation of Victorian London that she had often thought about with the Jekyll West End and the Hyde East End.

As such Rochester presented itself as a place of seeming: it seemed wealthy and yet had areas of poverty; it seemed historical and yet the historical was often manufactured; and it seemed safe whereas under the surface calm there were often violent undercurrents.

Charlie's car pulled up along side Catherine and she got in. Vicki was sitting in the back eating a slice of toast.

"Want some?" she said.

"No thanks I've had breakfast already, like about two hours ago."

"OK, sorry we're late. What's the plan for today? You strip whilst Charlie and me lynch the bastards?"

"For somebody whose just got out of bed she ain't half bubbling," thought Catherine, who offered a more practical way forward,

"If any of their mob are in the pub, Vicki, you chat one of them up and see if you can get them to take you back to their place, preferably the office. Charlie, you follow, first to make sure that she doesn't get into any trouble and secondly if they do go to any office or shop or warehouse you can break in and find out anything you can."

"This is going to be a bit of a long shot, Catherine. There are too many ifs, buts and maybes in this scheme of things," said Charlie.

"Can you think of anything better, because I can't?"

They agreed with this and she continued,

"Besides, I think we have to do something because they ain't going to hold back for much longer. The beatings are getting heavier. If we don't give way soon then one of us is going to get hurt pretty badly. I mean Pete only survived because he acted dead and played dumb."

"Not hard for him," said Vicki who had finished munching her toast and was licking the peanut butter from her fingers. Catherine turned round in her seat and in a reproachful voice said,

"Why can't you leave Pete alone? Why do you always have to have a go at him."

"Because I fancy him," she replied.

Charlie jumped in his seat and almost lost control of the car, it swerved and bumped up onto a curve before lurching back onto the road.

"Don't do that you plonker," he gasped. "Say something sensible would you?"

"As I said, I fancy him. It's just that I find it incredibly difficult to get through to him. I tried being nice once but he thought I was taking the piss and he dried up. So since then I've been nasty to him.

It seems to work, at least he takes notice of me now."

"Fuck me," said Catherine, "that's a bit of a revelation, what a turn up for Pete. Have you asked him out yet?"

"No, I'd thought I'd wait until this business is over. I mean he ain't going no place is he?"

The news took a little while to sink in. Charlie was definitely confused because Vicki was an extremely good looking blonde, with pale, watery blue eyes which always appeared to gaze abstractly before her. Her hair was shoulder length and was parted in the middle and then combed slightly forward at the front so that it gave her a girlish fringe. Her complexion was milky and her skin smooth. When she smiled her lips curled faintly on the left of her mouth giving her face a slightly quizzical look. Like Catherine she was fiercely intelligent and could wield words almost as effectively as Victor. She could, if she wanted to have her pick of men. That was how he reasoned. Catherine who knew something about Vicki's background could see why she might be drawn to the eccentric Pete but even so she could not resist the comment,

"But why Pete, he's not exactly your Kevin Costner is he?"

"Well, that's the fucking reason, ain't it. He's a moron like me. He's not your usual wham-bam-thank-you-mam type of bloke. I've had fucking problems with blokes like that in the past. You know I told you about my uncle, well he was one of those types, and after what he did to me I just don't feel like a macho-man."

"So there's hope for blokes like me yet," laughed Charlie who, although strong and powerfully built looked, as he put it, like the back end of a cow with diarrhoea. "What was that with your uncle? Do we know him? Do you want him done over?"

Vicki thought before replying and then measured out her words,

"My uncle, my fucking father's fucking brother, is a child molester. He gets his kicks out of little children. Or, to be exact about it, he gets it on from playing with eleven year old girls. He used to baby sit me when my mum was out on the evening shift, after my dad had pissed off from home. He used to have these games, like finding where he's hidden the one pound note. He'd hide it somewhere on his person and I'd have to try and find out where. I won't give you any prizes for guessing where he used to wrap it round?

"You are joking?" exclaimed Charlie.

"No I'm fucking well not. He'd tell me to look in his pockets and surprise, surprise, his trousers wouldn't be done up and they'd fall down and there it would be wrapped around his dick and held on with several elastic bands. So he'd make me pull off the bands one by one until I could unwrap the fucking money. One night he forced his prick into my mouth and I was sick."

"Why didn't you tell somebody?"

"I told my mum but she just hit me and told me to stop lying. You see Charlie, my mum was having a little affair with my uncle." Vicki's voice was now at its most sarcastic. "It was all in the family so to fucking well speak."

"No flipping wonder you left home at fifteen. Why didn't you tell the police or something?"

Charlie found it hard to accept that this could have gone on under a mother's protection; nature was being reversed. It was the everyday feeling about the incident from Vicki's past which evoked the greatest pathos.

"Oh yes, and be dragged through the courts as the kid who'd been molested. This was before the whole thing of incest had been opened up in the press."

Catherine joined in:

"I suppose you'd have got part of the blame. Perhaps not openly but it would still attach itself to you. People would talk about broken homes and all that and then you'd have those bloody interfering social workers trying to patch you up but only fucking you up instead. But I bet it goes on in posh homes as well, I bet it's wide spread. I bet there are some young girls now who are going through what you went through, with uncles or brothers, or even fathers. I've heard of blokes looking at their daughter in bloody unnatural ways after they've started to grow tits, fucking perverted. Some blokes are really screwed about sex. It's like that wanker of a judge who said that a woman who went out at night was asking for it. Funny how we get the blame."

"Yep. Anyway, when I was fourteen he busted me one Saturday night. My mum was out as normal and he'd come round and tried to persuade me to put on the new bikini that he'd bought me, but I wouldn't. So he threatened me and said he'd hurt me if I wasn't more grateful for the present. I thought I'd better put it on and when I came down again he was standing there without a stitch on, his ugly dick sticking up and he got me on the floor. My mum did fuck all about it except say he was a fine man and I'd have to lose my virginity some day. So a few months later I found this bundle of fivers on top of me mum's cupboard and I took it and left home. Any idea of romance, any thought of teenage love with all the hang-ups and frustrations, any thought of slowly experimenting with love and then sex were destroyed for me."

She paused for a moment before continuing,

"The strange thing is I don't want to be seen as a victim. I might be burning inside but I want to look life in the face. Anyway, joining the Class was a brilliant move because now I can really use my financial wizardry to good effect. So, to answer your third question, Charlie, if I could find him I'd love you for ever if you cracked his skull in."

A brief silence ensued broken by Vicki.

"So that's why I fancy Pete. He's a nice bloke."

She wanted to change the subject.

"So anyway what's this I heard about you in the health service being a raving red militant lunatic leftie shop steward Charlie? Dodgy motors and socialism don't mix very well do they?"

"Not really. No, I just worked in a hospital with an awful management who kept pushing us around so we thought we'd fight back. We almost won but what with these cut backs the pressure became too great and the other people got scared so they managed to sack me. After that they really hit the hospital, closing several wards down. But no, I'm not a raving red whatever you said shop steward, it's just that I kind of stumbled into being a shop steward."

"What, and stumbled into getting the sack?" asked Catherine. "Sounds to me that you got into more than you could handle."

"Nope, just the climate of the time. A lot of people were scared."

"Well, Mrs. T's gone now," grinned Vicki, "and now we've got that nice Mr. Major."

"We could have had that nice Mr. Kinnock if you lot had bothered to vote."

"What?" said Catherine, "Vote for a bloke who is going to take us further into Europe and destroy our heritage and hand our economy over to the Krauts? That's why people didn't vote for him. Who is going to vote for a party which says this country can't manage its own affairs and has to be bailed out by the German Blunderbunk."

"The what?" asked Vicki.

"The German big bank."

Charlie interrupted.

"Before we carry on setting the world to rights could somebody tell me where the Grapes is, because we are now coming into Southwark."

Inspector Benjamin was sitting on a public bench by Rochester Castle at Sunday lunchtime eating a sandwich and watching some children playing on the grass a few yards in front of him. This month was getting to be too hot for rapid police work and he sometimes mused how criminals could find the energy to commit their various crimes. He also started to think about the forthcoming cricket season and whether or not England would repeat its recent performances. Munching on his lunch he wished he were at some cricket ground this afternoon, preferably his favourite at Canterbury, sipping a pint, watching the runs pile up. He would sometimes not really watch the game at all, just sit there and enjoy the atmosphere. Still, the wanderings had to stop, he had several cases to close, particularly the child vice ring, and it was beginning to look as if Rochester's local alchy criminal was involved. That morning they had received a phone call from the Faversham police to say that a report had come in of two men being taken away from a video shop looking quite badly beaten up. Thankfully the local police had followed the instruction to phone through anything to do with videos in their local area. He had gone down to the shop owner who had said that the two men were local drunks who had got into a fight and had to be driven off by their friends. That did not sound at all plausible to Benjamin and the shop owner was definitely lying but nothing could be done about that. Two beatings concerning videos in one day was more than just coincidence. He would go and pay Victor a visit. Finishing his lunch he started to stroll down the castle walk and towards the other end of town. It being only a ten minute walk from the Castle to Troy Town where Victor lived he was there quite quickly and could not resist a smile when Victor opened his front door and stood there with a face which looked as if it had been used as a punch bag.

"Bloody hell, not you again."

Victor leaned against the door frame and stuck both his hands in his pockets in feigned resignation.

"Don't you lot ever give up?"

"Have you been in a fight then, or did you fall down the stairs or bang your face against the wardrobe door?"

"Look, it's Sunday afternoon and I was going to have a nice Sunday afternoon bloody kip and then you turn up. Make it quick."

"Where were you yesterday afternoon?"

"In Faversham," replied Victor who had decided to string along the police officer but not too much. "going about my lawful business."

"Anything happen?"

"I got mugged with a friend of mine just outside the video shop."

"Why didn't you report it."

"Listen, the number of times local people have been mugged and the police have said they can't do anything about it is getting to be too frequent. We didn't see the bloody point."

The explanation rang too true for Benjamin. Muggings and street crimes had increased an alarming degree over the past few years whilst convictions had slumped. Instinctively his police training took over his words.

"Yes, well, but if you members of the public don't let us know then how can we stop the violence. "

His wards rang hollow to him and he knew the sentiment was lost on Victor. He felt like a politician who is always saying that the end of the recession is in sight if only we tighten our belts a bit more. Joe Public stops believing it after a while and even worse starts to become cynical about the politician's intentions. It had become like that with police work. How much longer the public would accept excuses he didn't know, but the time was fast approaching when vigilantes would be on the streets protecting their own people and putting down opponents. New York coming to North Kent might have seemed stupid a few years ago, it might have seemed a nightmare in search of a dream, but to Benjamin the riots of the early '80s had started a change in law and order with the police on the losing side. His words had not convinced Victor who looked straight into Benjamin's eyes with a stare of disbelief which said 'don't patronise me, I'm not dumb.' However, the reply was a tired,

"Yes, well, look, I'm sorry we didn't report the incident but as you can see I'm just a little bit worn out and I really could do with a bit of a sleep."

"You didn't see your attackers?"

"No, the whole thing was too bloody quick."

It was a lost cause interrogating Victor and Benjamin turned to go down the steps.

"Let me know if anything turns up won't you?"

"Sure," said Victor who closed the door behind him, climbed the stairs to his flat and then sat in his throne thinking. A few minutes later there was another knock on his front door.

"Bloody hell," moaned Victor who slumped down the stairs ready to swear at the policeman. Instead he was greeted by a very pronounced South London accent.

"Excuse me, Mr. Manning."

It was John Wilson who spoke.

"That's me, the highly popular as it bloody well seems at the moment, Victor Manning."

"Well, we're sorry to bother you but we think we have something in common. Can we talk? It's about Nigel Croft-White and his mates."

The name did not register with Victor. Although what followed did,

"A very public school type of person who might just have paid you a visit."

The look of knowledge passed over Victor's face.

"Ah, I see that the bastard has already visited you."

"Yes, he's left his visiting card." Victor pointed to his facial bruising, "He after you as well?"

Arthur and John nodded.

"Well, you'd better come in."

John quickly explained their situation while Victor poured them both a drink. He got himself an orange juice.

"I'm on antibiotics," he explained handing Arthur his beer. "The whole thing is slowly making sense. They are obviously after video suppliers in Surrey and Kent. I bet they try and cut price some of the other dealers off the market. My girlfriend is up at the Grapes in Southwark finding out as much as she can about them. What is bothering us though is why they have decided to hit us, we ain't that big."

"That is why I reckon they are hitting the smaller blokes for something special," said John. "It's not the size of the business that's important, it's the spread. I wouldn't be surprised if they have gone North of the River as well. They have other interests, night clubs I think, but this interest in videos is something special. They were also very interested in the fact that you deal in video cameras and production."

"What, you think they might be going into film producing, 'Posh Bastards Films Incorporated'?"

"That's exactly what we think."

Victor was quickly beginning to understand the plan of Croft-White's operation.

"So what they do is they control the whole set-up, from the filming, to the processing, to the selling. That's quite clever, but they must be filming something pretty risky to have to go through all this. I mean, if they just wanted a complete bloody line of command they could have just bought a couple of shops themselves. That is the bit that is a bit bloody mysterious."

"I think it must be some sort of cover. It gives them some legitimacy."

Victor looked at Arthur and then at John with a gaze which spoke of confession time,

"I might as well bloody tell you that the word legitimate business does not really fit in very well around here. We are a little bit bloody shady."

"Well, let me shake your hand," said Arthur, "So are we."

"And because of that we are both vulnerable," said John who was putting aspects of their situation together very quickly indeed, "and because we are vulnerable we are subject to some sort of blackmail."

"Bloody hell, of course, they are hoping that we won't go to the police."

The three men chatted for the next half hour, agreeing in principle to work together and to pool their information. Ideas were exchanged and a partnership established. They talked quietly, attempting to agree a plan. But at the moment the most important missing factor was the motive of Croft- White and his firm. Victor brought the conversation to a conclusion.

"How about, if we wait until Catherine, Vicki and Charlie have found out what's going on and then I'll get Charlie to come and see you. Say Monday lunchtime."

They agreed and Arthur added,

"Come and see us at the Grapes. I think I'd like to bring the landlord in on this. Once he sees that people with enough clout are moving against Nigel Croft-White he might just swing a few more our way."

"What if the posh bastard turns up for a drink?"

"He won't. He never comes in on a Monday, he has some business up in London."

They agreed that Charlie would come and see them on Monday and with a final shake of hands Arthur and John left with more peace of mind than they had had for many days.

Chapter 13

"Sorry darling, we can't use you. Our regular dancer turned up. We phoned your agent about an hour ago. Seems you came in for nothing. Still have a drink on the house, you and your two friends, have a drink."

"That's decent of you," replied Catherine. "most landlords would have said 'bye-bye'."

"Ah, not the Grapes, we like pretty girls. Might be able to use you next Friday night. There's a stag do, about fifty blokes, somebody is getting married or something. Fancy entertaining the lads then?"

Catherine rarely turned down a job but on this occasion a stag night at a South London pub was not going to be fun. She was also not sure about the timing of the next film set.

"No thanks, we'll just have our drinks."

The three of them sat down in the crowded pub.

"Finished at the starting post," said Charlie. "What the fuck do we do now?"

"Get pissed," replied Vicki.

"I'm being serious."

"So was I. Although I have to say it, I don't like this pub, it's too large. Looks as if it might have had a few punch ups in its time."

"It also looks as if it could do with a decent regular dancer. Christ that old dear must be about thirty if she's a day."

Catherine had looked across the bar at the stage which was larger and more decorated than the stage at the Lamb and Flag. It also had a DJ at the back of it getting ready to play a tape as the dancer moved to the front of the audience. She danced to a Blondie track; 'good choice,' thought Catherine, 'shame about the girl'.

"I bet they only use one girl here," she said above the sound of the music. "Fatal. Poor girl will run out of ideas by the third dance. Actually, to look at her, she'll probably run out of ideas half way through this one."

Indeed, the dancer did not look very inspirational and was repeating the sequence of movements for the second time. The drinkers looked happy enough although Catherine thought they were playing at being entertained in case their drinking buddies thought they weren't interested in seeing a woman dance her way to nudity.

The landlord was encouraging them with cheers and calls of 'get-em-off.' Charlie was about to stand up and move towards the bar for a better look when Vicki pulled him down and cried,

"Hey, you militant tendency socialist, I thought this stuff is meant to be sexist? Aren't you supposed to walk out or something?"

"God, I wish I'd never said I was once a shop steward. I just want a little look, all right?" He was at the bar now with the rest of the men.

"He'll end up an MP at this rate," said Catherine remembering her own club-land experience.

"Yeah, we could campaign on the slogan, 'put a Charlie in parliament. One more won't make any difference'."

After the dance Charlie returned and sat down. The girl took a couple of minutes break and then started again. Catherine was amazed.

"What is she trying to do, break the strip speed record? That will turn the punters right off."

Charlie and Catherine started to have a discussion about the eroticism of the strip tease whilst Vicki looked around her. She was conscious of being eyed by some rather drunk men in the corner. She ignored their gaze. In the Lamb and Flag she would have gone up to them with 'you got a problem or something?', but in an unfamiliar pub it was best to keep quiet. Besides which it was about time they left before Charlie had drunk too much to get them back safely. However, one of the men came over from the corner and lurched towards her.

"Hello darling, all on your own then?" it said. The accent definitely did not fit in with Southwark.

'Here we go again,' thought Vicki to herself.

Charlie looked aggressively towards the man,

"No, she's with me."

"Greedy bounder aren't you, two girlies at once. Nice." The voice was clipped and the vowels were precise.

"Why don't you piss off," said Vicki in a voice loud enough for the landlord to hear. She guessed that he'd come in to help them before Charlie took a swing at the bloke. Charlie had indeed started to stare aggressively in front of him, not looking at the owner of the voice but concentrating on a spot by the door. His fists were slowly and deliberately being clenched.

"Common little thing. Does common little girl want to come ride in big man's Rolls-Royce?" The voice's friends were leering in their direction, the landlord did not move but looked concerned.

"Listen wanker, if you don't back off I'll crack this fucking bottle across your head."

Vicki picked up a bottle from the next table and cradled it, it was more of a threat than anything. She'd been in this situation hundreds of times and knew how to act against real drunks. Normally, the drunk would have backed away with a curse to rejoin his friends, to leer some more but not to interfere again. This one was more persistent.

"Why don't you dance for us, a blondie dancing to a Blondie tape." He laughed at his witticism and the rest of his friends joined in. The regulars in the pub stopped drinking and looked at the voice. Charlie got up with fist clenched, angry and ready for a fight. The voice's companions moved towards him, nobody in the pub tried to stop them.

"Come on girlie, £40 if you dance for us. Or you gorgeous," it said looking at Catherine, "£40 if you dance for us."

The landlord called out,

"She's a dancer, that one with the dark hair. She'll do it."

He looked at Catherine with a desperate stare as if she could get his pub out of a violent fight.

"Don't fucking do it," said Vicki, "fuck 'em, they're wankers."

Charlie was ready to smash a fist into the voice's face and Vicki, who had broken the bottom of the bottle was about to slash with it when Catherine put her arm around her shoulder and pulling tightly towards her whispering,

"Back off, I think I know who these blokes are. Public school accents in Southwark. It's not just coincidence."

She called out,

"Right, make it £50 and I'll be your second dancer for this afternoon. Two strips each. That OK, deary?"

The other girl shouted her agreement over the din of welcoming cheers. Drinkers made their way to the bar to get refills before the dance started whilst Catherine was manoeuvred through the crowd to the back of the bar to a small room so that she could change. The landlord went with her and closed the door behind them.

"That's done it," he said. "I hope you're good at it."

"I'm the best," replied Catherine. "The absolute best. I also got you out of a scrape. My boyfriend is pretty handy with his fists."

"I could see that, so thanks a lot. We've had a bit of trouble here recently with that mob by the door. Not our kind. Anyway, I'll leave you to get changed, here's your £50 from the loud mouth with the posh accent and here's an extra tenner from me. By the way, we have a rule that you have to keep your knickers on until the last dance."

"A professional dancer always does. Keeps the punters guessing."

The landlord left convinced that Catherine knew what she was doing, the first girl walked out to do another dance while Catherine changed into her black outfit. In fact the first dancer had finished just as she was adding the final touches. Catherine looked up at her as she walked in.

"That was quick," she said.

"No point in hanging around here darling. Bunch of bastards out there."

The drinkers in the bar were calling for her, and when she walked out and slinked onto the stage the cheering was wild. She teased and taunted them before starting the dance, showing just enough to cultivate the interest. Strip-tease as she knew was more about the tease than the strip. The music started, Heart of Glass by Blondie.

"Must be the DJ's favourite band," she mused.

For her first routine she used the slow and sensual approach, the raunchy would be the second dance. She moved around the large stage and looked at the men. They were an older audience so she'd have to go slower and allow them to imagine what their wives were once like. There was one old man smiling at her who looked as if he wanted to come up on stage with her, he was imitating every move that she made. She took off her bra and he acted out the same movements, she fondled her breasts and he did likewise, she swept her hands up through her hair and above her head and he did the same. The other old men were loving it, some were reeling about, laughing in a drunken hysterical state.

"OK, old boy, try this," she said to herself.

She turned around and spread her legs wider and wider, until she was doing the splits, her buttocks were swaying and thrusting upwards. She looked through the widening gap between her legs to see what he was doing and there he was trying to do the splits, the men in the crowd watching him as well as watching her. Then he lost his balance, waving his arms in the air, trying to grab hold of something he fell over knocking two other old geezers to the ground. A huge cheer went up. She continued to dance and was gently rubbing between her legs whilst slowly starting to rise. The old boy was on his feet again but was no longer following her, he was standing there cheering with the rest. The dance lasted for a further five minutes and Catherine managed to make it to the bar before the punters had realised that she was finished. Back in the room she slumped onto a chair breathing deeply. The first dancer looked at her.

"You take a bit of a risk doing that kind of dance here. It's a rough bar you know."

"I'm used to it."

"I could see that. I was impressed with the way you handled those posh bastards in the corner. I thought your boyfriend was going to kill Nigel."

"Who?"

"The bloke who spoke. They're a pretty hard bunch and not very popular around here."

Catherine was dressing again for her second dance and knew that this was an opportunity for finding out something. The drinkers were getting rowdy, calling for more.

"I'm not going out there," said the dancer, "It's getting out of hand."

"Doesn't bother me."

"Fucking hell, you must love it rough darling. You must fucking love it."

"Yeah," said Catherine, "tell me about those posh blokes. Any of them good for a few quid, show 'em a good time and all that."

"You a tart too?"

"Yeah, I live by sex. Tell me about them."

"Well..." the dancer was changing into her normal clothes when the landlord came in.

"You ready yet?"

"I ain't going on. Not with them lot in that mood. Give me my money please."

The landlord gave her half the amount.

"You don't do the full amount you don't get the full amount," he explained.

"You fucking bastard," she said. Catherine placed her hand on his shoulder and said,

"Come on give her the cash. We're only working girls and you know I can get them going. It wouldn't be fair to expect her to go out into that."

The landlord put his hands in his pockets and reluctantly handed over the rest of the money before shutting the door behind him shouting to the drinkers to expect Catherine back.

"Listen deary, thanks, I need that cash. I'll do something for you some day." She put on her coat and made ready to leave.

"You can do something for me now. Tell me about the posh blokes."

"Oh, them," she leant up against the door. "Public school types, West End. They have a video suppliers shop up by the Elephant. Heavy types and a bit kinky. They might be legit or dodgy, I don't really know, but they certainly run this pub and the landlord is shit scared of them. 'Bye darling and thanks."

The girl slipped through the door and out through the back passage. A rhythmical stamping came from the pub followed by chanting,

"We want pussy, we want pussy."

Catherine looked through a chink in the door. The expression on the faces of the men were changed. They were far gone, well pissed and the alcohol was changing the atmosphere in there. Gone was the high spirited 'all lads together' of the normal pub strip. It had been replaced by a far more menacing feeling, one of potential trouble, the real macho sexuality. Catherine had seen this before and knew that it would take everything that she had to keep this under control. The landlord couldn't and as far as she could see he had no bouncers.

"Into the valley of death," she breathed as she quickly walked through the door and into the bar.

She never reached the stage. One man grabbed her round the waist and pulled her towards him and another held her right leg. Some old bloke was trying to kiss her and she felt her bra being undone. She knew exactly what to do and took a sudden dive coming to her feet again tightly holding two men's testicles and squeezing hard. They screamed in agony. She could see Charlie and Vicki throw themselves into the crowd around her but before they could reach her the bloke with the posh voice and his three heavies had flung themselves at the group of drinkers and had shoved them all to the ground leaving Catherine standing with two blokes leaning up against her begging her to let go. She did. Vicki could not resist retaliation and aimed a kick at one of the men now sinking to the ground. It caught him in the stomach and he doubled up in pain.

"I say, nice shot old girl," said the voice, "ever played football?"

"I'll play football with one of their fucking heads in a minute," she said.

The voice took command of the situation.

"OK, everyone, the fun's over. You can get back to your drinking. Landlord, everyone is to have a drink on me."

The bruised male egos accepted this peace offering, trouble with the voice was not recommended. The pub quickly returned to normal as Charlie led Catherine to the back room to get changed. The landlord was quickly serving drinks whilst the voice was chatting to Vicki.

"Wonderful show, pretty young thing. I say, don't you think we could be friends? I mean we did do something to help. My name's Nigel."

Vicki could not believe the good fortune. This was going to be easy.

"Well, OK, you can buy me a drink, but I don't like being called common. My name's Sharon."

'Why did I think of that one,' she thought. 'Talk about common and unimaginative to boot.' Nigel laughed and they sat down.

"I won't make any comment about your name, although I must say..."

"Yes, I know, it's common. OK? I didn't choose it," she slammed her fist in mock annoyance on the table and continued, "listen I want to go and see my two friends and see how they are. You get the drinks. I want a brandy."

"Large or small?" he asked as she got up.

"Bloody enormous!" she replied.

Charlie and Catherine were getting ready to leave when Vicki told them what had happened.

"Right into our laps," said Catherine.

"We got there after all," added Charlie, "a bit of a round about route and a bit dangerous but we got there."

"Right," Vicki was taking command now, "I want you two to piss off. Don't trail me Charlie, I won't need you. The pair of you had better leave quickly in case any of the regulars want a return match against Catherine. Walk out the front and say thanks to the posh bloke, who is called Nigel by the way. And, oh yes, I almost forgot, I changed my name to Sharon."

She paused whilst Catherine burst into a stifled laugh.

"You what?"

"And I'm going to call you Debbi and you Richard. All right?"

"All right Tracy," said Charlie.

Vicki looked at him in an exasperated fashion and gently cuffed him across the chin.

"I said Sharon."

"Why do we have to change our names?"

"Just in case they know of a threesome who happen to be called Catherine, Charlie and Vicki, you wally. They've already hit a Dave and a Pete and a Victor, haven't they."

Charlie tapped his head and said,

"Sorry. Brain not functioning at the moment."

They moved rapidly out of the room and to the corner where Nigel and his friends were.

"Everything fine?" enquired Nigel.

"Yes, thanks very much. My name's Debbi and this is Richard. If you ever need a stripper for a private party with well behaved guests look me up."

Charlie nodded in thanks and half waved his good-byes. They left and were not followed by any of the drinkers.

"So Sharon, how are you now? Absolutely fine? Not too bruised or anything?"

"I'm feeling just great Nigel. Just one thing though. I really don't want three other blokes sat there looking gormless and like three spare pricks at a wedding. Don't you think we could find a quieter pub for a little get-to-know-you-chat?"

"Good idea. How about my place?"

Vicki was ready to say yes but her instinct told her not to move too fast.

"You're a bit forward aren't you?" she said. "I'm not that sort of a girl. A pub first. Well actually I'd like something to eat, something decent."

"I know just the place," he reflected.   "Quite quiet and jolly.
Let's go."

She drank her brandy in one gulp and it really was a large one and
Nigel muttered some instructions to his cronies before he put his arm
around her shoulder and led her out of the front door.

They walked in the slight drizzle towards the car which was a
Rolls-Royce and had another heavy leaning up against it. Vicki was
impressed and thought to herself,

'These bunch of bastards really are creaming off some money.'

"I'm impressed," she said looking up at him acting out her role
like a star from a Mills and Boon story.

'I'll put on such a performance that Catherine will give me an
Oscar,' she continued thinking to herself.

"Why the bloke with the muscles?"

Nigel pulled her closer towards himself and said,

"What a naive pretty young thing you are.   First of all, he's my
chauffeur and secondly I would not want to leave my lovely car
around here and find that the wheels had been removed by the time I
got back."

Vicki giggled as he opened the door for her.

"Silly me. OK, Jeeves, drive on."

Nigel shut the door and walked around to the other side.   He sat
beside her and patted her knee.

"And now my lovely I now this super unpretentious Italian
restaurant in WC 1"

"OK, let's go," she said.   "Oh look, a drinks' cabinet. Mine's a
brandy."

Chapter 14

Victor was sitting in his throne, leaning slightly forward and listening to what Catherine and Charlie were telling him. He concentrated his thoughts on the subject as powerfully as a chess grandmaster might over a complicated opening variation, his eyes were tunnelling a hole in the floor just before him, his brows rigidly fixed, his lips compressed together. The Lawyer listened too, as if contemplating his reply to the bosses opening gambit and was leaning back against the window with his chin resting on one of his hands.

"We take some risks with our people," Victor said, "I hope Vicki knows exactly what she's doing."

"Of course she does," replied Catherine. "As far as that posh bastard is concerned she's just a grateful and common young slut, who likes to take a ride in a Rolls-Royce, who likes good food and who likes getting pissed and then getting laid. Remember, that's what they've been taught at their public schools: there are good girls who talk properly and who act sweetly and charmingly and who they can marry and there are bad girls who didn't go to the right schools, who talk common and who can be bought for a cheap thrill. They like to stereotype women. That posh bastard won't have a clue about Vicki or what she's about. She'll have him in the palm of her hand."

"I think that might be a little bit sweeping Cathy, public schools have changed a bit you know. Mind you, that's only recently so you might be right," said the Lawyer. "I met some of them public school types at my one term at university. They were pathetic. They used to turn up to social events and stand around in groups giving the women marks out of ten as they walked in."

"You what?" exclaimed Victor. "We got over that by the end of our first year at secondary school."

Catherine was pouring another drink and smiling at Victor waving a bottle of beer at him and wagging her finger as if to say 'not for you'. She handed the Lawyer his beer and Victor his glass of orange juice.

"Yes, well, lover, but then you see there are some blokes who don't get over that sort of thing until their second year of retirement."

Their conversation was interrupted by the telephone ringing.

Catherine answered it:

"Hello. Oh hello Sharon. How's lover boy... Good... You'll be back tomorrow... Good... Good... Good... Yes I've got that written down... Be a good girl... 'Bye..."

Catherine ripped the sheet of paper from the pad and waved it in the air.

"She's done it! She's actually done it! It only took her four hours. The posh bastard is in the bathroom so she 'phoned through the address of the warehouse. We've got to raid the place. We hit it tonight. Fuck me!"

"Not with all these people around, Catherine," Victor said, "later, certainly." He got up from his chair and shouted, "We've got the bastards. We move tonight. Lawyer, get hold of Dave and Louise and bring your van around. Charlie, bring yours too. Pete, you'll drive the car. We'll need three vehicles on this one. OK, let's move. I want everyone here by midnight."

They left the flat and Victor moved across to Catherine.

"Now, what did you say about wanting to be fucked?"

"Anytime lover, but are sure your bruises will allow you to..."

She didn't finish her sentence. Victor had picked her up and carried her towards the bed, dropping her onto the mattress he lay on top of her and looked into her eyes.

"There's one part of me that ain't bruised!" he said.

"Victor, how original," she giggled and wriggled from under him. "I want a shower first. Come and have one with me."

She moved towards the bathroom swinging her hips whilst Victor fell off the bed and followed her on all fours, bounding along like a dog. He reached up and held her round the waist, pulling himself up whilst pulling her skirt down. His chin was on her shoulder, his lips were kissing her neck and his hands were slowly undressing her. She turned around and playfully bit his ear.

"It's nice to be undressed," she whispered.

His hands were on her buttocks, gently massaging them to-and-fro.

"I always knew you were into massage, right from the first time," she continued, "I like the way you use your mouth on the upper regions and you... ouch... what are you doing down there?"

Victor had taken off her knickers and had buried his tongue into her vagina, moving it backwards and forwards, licking and probing, gently pulling on her pubic hairs, rubbing himself against her clitoris.

"Fuck me," she gasped, "I've heard of French kissing..."

She always chatted through their love making, until near the end when gasps replaced syllables. Victor slowly stood up, running his face up from her belly and over her breasts, gently caressing her nipples with his lips. He had penetrated her now and was thrusting deeper into her and all the time kissing and licking her neck.

"I want topsies," she said as she pushed him to the floor and he allowed her to roll on top of him.

She pinned him to the ground moving herself backwards and forwards, squirming over him, rotating her hips in a gentle and slightly circular fashion and writhing with delight. The moment came when desire succeeded everything and Victor's eyes blazed with lust. She was leaning away from him, her back arched, her hands grasping his knees, she started to groan and Victor shuddered as he shot himself into her. She held that position for several seconds more, her head tilted back, hair flowing down her swan-like neck. She gave one last gasp and leant forward, looking full into Victor's twinkling eyes. He had his hands behind his head and had a smug expression on his face.

"You don't often come down on me," he whispered.

Catherine uttered a long breathy exclamation,

"Fuck me."

"Again? OK."

They made love in the shower, in the bed and on Victor's chair.

"I'll say one thing about these pain killers," said Victor.

"What?"

"They ain't pleasure killers."

They both laughed and got dressed.

"You know what I'd like to do one day?" said Catherine.

"No, tell me."

"I'd like to spend a weekend down in Brighton, in a seedy hotel, during a rain swept February. And I'd like to walk along the sea front as illicit lovers with the landlady watching us, tutt-tutting. You know, the way they did it in the fifties and sixties, all that risk taking; sex has become definitely too safe, enjoyable but definitely not enough risk. Yes, I'd like an old fashioned dirty weekend."

"What on earth gave you that idea? Have they been showing sixties films on the telly again? It sounds distinctly kinky. Besides which landladies don't tutt-tutt any more. And if it's risky sex you want stand at the top of Star Hill and pick up a bloke, charge him twenty quid and don't use any protection. That sounds pretty risky to me."

"Not that sort of risk, more like when we were teenagers, you know, trying to get laid in the most public places without getting caught."

"You what? You've never told me about this."

"I did, when you were pissed about a year ago. I told you about my first boyfriend who was into that sort of thing."

"Where was the most public place you did it then?" enquired Victor.

"The law courts in Maidstone."

"You bloody well didn't, did you?"

"Yes we bloody well did. No one around of course. Now that was risky." Catherine placed her arms around her lover's neck, "And then I'd like to spend a weekend at the Savoy."

"Now that sounds more like it. We'll do it but in the meantime, you know what I'd like?"

"Tell me."

"I'd like a drink."

Catherine pushed him back onto his throne and sat on his lap.

"Come on, you know what the doctor said, not until Tuesday."

The pair of them chatted for the next minutes about nothing in particular and about everything in general. They had reached the point in their relationship where they could either spend hours together saying nothing or could talk the night away. As on previous occasions when the Class had had to act as one for protection the conversation was desultory, roving from one subject to another, without really connecting; it was a style which betrayed a certain nervousness and apprehension. Vicki would have done her homework thoroughly and would not have allowed them to chance a confrontation unless she knew that the warehouse was going to be left unguarded, but even so this was not a job which either of them relished completing. There was always a feeling of risk in their line of business, even though both were almost legitimate. Catherine had on a couple of occasions helped Victor import some uncensored videos and had dealt in some recording equipment which was definitely not acquired legally. He had always operated on the borderline between success and failure and this time he might just be pushed over the line to where the losers of society existed.

Victor knew that they could take on this new threat. It seemed to him that there existed a certain contradiction in the way the posh bastards operated. The area of their interests was decidedly down market. They could well take over the Class's interests if no resistance was put up, but if tonight's operation was a success then they could well back off and try easier targets. It was finding out exactly what they were up to that was important. If Vicki could get further information then the whole thing could be ended quite quickly before they had time to regroup.

The other threat to the Class would be if the police became involved, if they realised that this break-in was not just an act of burglary but part of a revenge and protection movement. So far the police had nothing really definite on the Class and Victor wanted to keep it that way. Once they started to investigate deeper than just the surface they could start to put a great deal of pressure on them. It was unlikely that in today's climate the police would adopt the attitude of it being two firms fighting it out and therefore keeping clear. They would move in hard and Victor feared that the posh bastards could bluff it out, trading on background and possible past respectability whilst all that the Class had to present to the world were a bunch of secondary modern school failures combining a dodgy motor dealer, a video dealer and a stripper. He was taking a risk, not being sure whether the child porn ring was connected with this lot, if they were then the Class might just have to break cover and shop the bastards to the police. But that might mean exposing their operation and it was not a risk he was prepared to take at the moment. As far as possible the Class did not show its face, it waited for the moment to strike and then moved in hard, getting what it wanted and then quickly getting out. A set piece battle with the forces of law and order was not a good idea.

So they chatted for about an hour, discussing the various options until Victor lent back in his throne and said,

"'Ere, you know what you said about risky sex?"

"Yes, lover."

"Well put your jacket on we're going for a walk."

Catherine giggled.

"Where to?"

"Up the top of Star Hill."

Catherine looked startled,

"Victor Manning what have you got in store for me? You ain't effing well selling me." She had her hands on her hips in mock annoyance, "I ain't a tart and you ain't an effing pimp. Besides which I've got some little rubber friends so it wouldn't be that risky."

"Oh bloody well calm down lust of my life. Get your coat on and let's go."

They walked down the stairs to the front door and Catherine spun round.

"Why are we going to the top of Star Hill? We ain't going to do it in that court yard are we."

"Nope."

"Well, what about by that old closed down club."

"Nope. Not public enough."

Catherine giggled as they walked through the doorway.

"I know, we're going to do it on the traffic island right in the middle."

Victor looked at her with a withering expression.

"I thought risk was your kink, not bloody suicidal. Nope, come on."

They walked arm in arm to the top of Star Hill and crossed the road to the grassy hill on the other side.

"See that old covered seats type thing up there?"

"Oooooo," muttered Catherine, "We ain't going to do it there are we?"

"Yep."

Victor grabbed her by the waist and in the dark they moved silently and expectantly towards their makeshift love nest. On reaching the seats they sank down into the gloom hoping that the darkness was sufficient to cover them like a blanket.

"Victor, lover?" hummed Catherine.

"Yes."

"Start from the top and work down this time."

Victor started to slip his hand down her side to the base of her tee-shirt and was slowly raising it, whilst with the other hand he drew her face towards his, ready to kiss. They never got any further. Three figures loomed out of the darkness from the other side of the structure and stared at the lovers.

"Hey man, wild sex," said one of the dishevelled men, lurching forwards.

Both Victor and Catherine were on their feet, Catherine glaring threateningly at the small group of trampishly dressed young men. Victor's eyes flashed hatred.

"Who the bloody hell are you?" he uttered in a low gutteral voice.

"Cool man, cool. We're travellers. Hey come to a party down at the camp. Rave up and..."

He got no further. Victor's hatred for hippies flared dramatically and with one punch straight to the traveller's lower chest he set the man doubling up, gasping for breath, his chokes sounding as if they were a death rattle. The other two looked shocked and stunned.

"Leave off man, we ain't done no harm. Just looking."

Victor shouted at them and jabbed a finger with each word.

"I don't like bloody travellers, I don't like bloody hippies and I don't like wankers who destroy people's homes with their bloody camps."

The two hippies stared in pained and stunned and hazed disbelief, their reactions slowed by what they had taken earlier. One of them slouched in a supplicatory fashion towards Catherine who moved towards him and breathed,

"And I don't like fucking junkies!"

She went down on one knee and grabbed him by the testicles, coming up sharply she sent him backwards falling onto the ground and then smashed a heel into his teeth.

"Now, you bloody wanker, let me give you good warning. If you lot come to Rochester and disrupt our lives I swear blind that there are enough of us to bloody well hurt you lot."

He held the hippy round the neck in a powerful grip.

"Understand," he said twisting the grip tighter.

The hippy choked with tears in his eyes and managed a plea for mercy. Victor twisted the grip tighter.

"I said: do you understand?"

"Yes," choked the man.

Victor let him fall to the ground. The young man crawled to his friends who lay in agony. Victor continued,

"You see wanker, you might get protection from the law, you

might scrounge on the dole but the time is coming when the people are going to take the law into their own hands and drive you bastards out. We've had enough of you wankers. Get my drift?"

He aimed a kick at the prostrate youth.

"I said, get my drift?"

The hippy assented by nodding his head and wimpering a reply which was inaudible. The hippy whom Catherine had felled made to get up. Moving quickly towards him she grabbed him by the hair, pulled him towards her and kneed him sharply several times in the face. He collapsed.

"Brilliant lover," she said as they walked away, "Almost as good as a fuck."

She punched a fist in the air, turned round at the three travellers and shouted,

"People power, people vigilantes, fuck the hippies."

They crossed the road and began to walk down Star Hills.

"It might just come to that you know," Victor said, "vigilantes, bloody great."

"Fucking brilliant."

"I'm hungry."

"For sex or food?"

"Both. Food first. We'll need something to eat before tonight's little raid."

"The Lamb and Flag will be open in a couple of minutes."

The two lovers sauntered towards the pub with a glowing feeling inside of them; they felt themselves to be invincible after the fight, they felt themselves in control of events. They pushed open the door of the pub and went inside.

After the mauling the three travellers had received from Victor and Catherine they went back to the camp and talked to the tall gaunt youth.

"You'd better go and see Brownslow," he said. "Pretty heavy to me."

Brownslow was emptying some rubbish into a huge bin at one end of the field when the news was broken to him.

"Well," he droned, "What can we do? You want to go back and sort them out? I fucking well don't. They are too far away and too insignificant for me. Like some distant planet going nowheres."

The gaunt youth looked at him with staring, blurred eyes.

"What about the heavy violence against the girl this afternoon?"

"It ain't fucking on," said Brownslow, "It ain't fucking on. Croft-White wants any help from us he ain't going to get it."

"Getting too bloody violent," said the gaunt youth, "Too bloody heavy."

Chapter 15

By midnight they had all assembled, by two o'clock they had completed the plans and were ready to move off: Louise, Dave and Victor in the car; Charlie and Catherine in the first van and the Lawyer and Pete in the second. Pete had brought a baseball bat with him.

"Just in case I get the chance of a grudge match against the bloke what done me over," he explained. "This is better than a cricket bat."

"It's the one decent thing the Yanks have invented then," replied the Lawyer. "I think the general idea is Pete that we avoid violence at this stage. Any trouble and we go. They'll bring in the police if they spot us, that is if they are at all clever."

"Except McDonalds'," reasoned Pete who had not caught up with the explanation on avoiding violence.

"Pardon? What about McDonalds'?"

"They invented McDonalds' as well as baseball bats."

The Lawyer looked across at Pete bemused.

"Yes, all right they invented McDonalds'. But I hardly think that the invention of fast food increased the sum total of civilisation."

"And TV dinners."

"Yes, OK, and TV dinners."

"And Budweiser."

Pete was not going to stop in his listing of the American achievements.

"And frizzbees... and Westerns.... and Walt Disney... and..." he was interrupted.

"Now there I grant you was an invention worth mentioning, Walt Disney. However Pete, seeing as Charlie has just moved off in the van ahead and seeing as Louise is beeping her horn behind us don't you think we could make tracks?"

The ignition was started and the van moved off. Pete was an exceptionally fine driver and could handle any motor at whatever speed. The small convoy headed towards London with respectable gaps between the vehicles, they did not want to get stopped by any police car. In the car Victor thought of the film The Italian Job and

the small minis bounding and bouncing through the buildings of
Rome. He hoped that their enterprise would not be as comic or as
close to disaster as Michael Caine's small band of villains was. He
thought of the car chases he'd seen in countless gangster movies and
trusted that they'd get away unseen and not followed. He thought of
the comical trap set by Alec Guinness and Stanley Holloway in The
Lavender Hill mob and prayed that they weren't walking into trouble.
But paramount in his mind was the thought of the gun and possible
shootings. He felt the cut-throat blade in his pocket and thought to
himself:

'It might be passe, or whatever that posh bastard had said it was,
but it's still quick and clean and easy to wield. Give me a blade to cut
with and a pair of brogues to kick with and I'll take on any bastard,
gun or no gun.'

Victor had never succumbed to the current fashion of wearing
D.M.'s for fights. They were too heavy to swing and weighed you
down if you had to run fast. He had preferred the early seventies
style of full leather brogues with Blakey studs in the heels. A kick
with one brogue would bring any one down and then when they were
on the ground grind the heel into their face. It made a real mess, it
would knock out a set of front teeth in a few seconds. He had
developed his art of fighting to a high level; the D.M. toe was too
rounded to cause maximum damage, the airware sole too cushioned to
hurt badly and besides which the brogue looked smarter. He'd learnt
all this from an older friend who was one of the heavies in the early
seventies and he had liked the style, the smartness, the almost over-
the-top immaculate dress sense: the crombies with the legendary silk
hankie in the top pocket, trilbies, the Ben Shermans and the suits. It
was the kind of style which appealed to him. He stretched himself out
on the back seat and mumbled one of the chants from that era:

"Jump up off your knees, kick him in the bollocks.
"Jump up off your knees, kick him in the head.
"Jump up off your knees, kick that fucking hippie.
"Kick that fucking hippie,
"Till that hippie's fucking dead."

Dave turned round and looked quizzically at him,

"I don't think it's hippies that we're up against Victor. I think
they're public school types, or have you finally gone vacant up
stairs?"

"No, I was just thinking about a time gone by."

"Eh? Don't you think you ought to be concentrating upon the era just about to come upon us? You know, the breaking and entering era."

"It just helps to prepare me. This is going to be a quick and clean operation, get in and get out, fast."

The streets were almost deserted as they sped along, entering London within an hour. Where London started and Surrey finished was hard to tell, but as soon as they entered Morden and then went on to Kennington there was a perceptible change of atmosphere in the surroundings. There was a constant sense of change about South London, an area which had grown later than North of the River. It still had the feel of crumbling Victorian power about it, the buildings had not yet achieved the uniform bleakness of Newham or Tower Hamlets. The council blocks by the Elephant and Castle stood like sentinels on their slightly rising hill and the longer and straighter roads facilitated a faster movement. It was as if people could escape from this part of London if they wanted to, it had none of the claustrophobia of Camden or the isolation of Hackney. The area south of the Thames had crumbled as one and had not managed to retain the distinctive village structure of North London. There were a few enclaves of prosperity but by and large the district had surrendered its former grandeur with only a few sighs and even fewer regrets. It was a gateway to something else; to the North was the excitement of the West End, to the south was Kent and, increasingly, the continent. It was a place of transition rather than stability and a place where movement rather than rest was the main condition of life. There was no real centre of power here, if all roads north of the river led to Westminster and Central London, then all roads in the south led nowhere except away. The community had fragmented quickly during the seventies and eighties with each of the racial groups going their separate ways. If the place was to be compared with any other metropolitan centre then it would be to New York, with the minority groups becoming the majority and with municipal mismanagement and bankruptcy. Like New York very few people who had not lived there could understand its particular problems, nor the desperate actions of hard left politicians who were involved with certain councils. The area had become the poor neighbour of the north without the north's tourist attractions or cultural facilities or financial centres. In short,

South London had slowly become something of a national joke; to live in Lambeth was to court ridicule, to live in New Cross or Catford was to receive sympathy. It was a situation resented by people who had been born there and who felt powerless to reverse the decline.

The three vehicles swept through Kennington and up to the Elephant and Castle. They turned in to a side street on the corner of which was a demolished building. The warehouse stood at the end of this street next to some rented garages, a small waste land which looked like having the makings of an unofficial rubbish tip and opposite a half knocked down graffiti scrawled wall. A small side street bordered the warehouse and they parked their vehicles just by the entrance. There were no lights in the building, which was on the small size for a major operation. Dave looked around for any alarm systems and found what he was looking for.

"This won't take too long," he said as he set to work, "quite old fashioned in many ways."

The wiring system was indeed out of date and within two minutes Dave had successfully shorted it and cut off any possible alarm. Charlie forced a window and then used his hydraulic press to force apart the bars. He climbed through, followed by Catherine, Louise and Dave. Pete looked up at the small gap through the window and then down at his belly.

"Shall I stand guard over the vehicles?" he said to Victor.

"No need. They'll open the doors in a minute or two." Inside Charlie had started to force the door from the inside whilst the others looked around the darkened room. There were boxes everywhere. Catherine ripped one open and inside were about fifty videos. She read out a couple of titles:

"Sweet Thirteen... Now I Am Six... If They Are Old Enough To Bleed, They Are Old Enough To Fuck..."

Charlie forced the door when a crash was heard from inside the warehouse. Catherine had in anger pushed over a column of about six boxes that had been standing at the back sending videos scattering across the floor. She kicked one towards Victor who had come in looking worried in case there had been an accident. Catherine spat out her words.

"These are fucking child sex videos. We're dealing with a bunch of fucking child molesters."

Her anger penetrated the night atmosphere charging the other members of the Class with hatred. No body spoke until Louise ripped open another box.

"Fucking hell, here's more. Let's burn the fucking place to the ground."

Pete was swinging his baseball bat around him and then started to aim at the boxes. Victor ripped open a couple more that were nearer the door.

"They've mixed legitimate copies with the sick ones," he said. "Right, we move quick. Get all of these loaded. Pete get that trolley and shift the bigger ones."

They all moved as one, organising themselves into a chain, handing each box along the line whilst Charlie stood on board the first lorry stacking them in a corner. Pete trundled boxes, sweat was soaking his shirt but he didn't notice. The boxes on one side of the room were shifted and then Charlie backed off the full lorry as Pete drove the second one into place. They carried on working, a bit slower now that they had settled into a routine. Louise walked down the street to make sure that nobody was around. It was deserted. Within half an hour the building was clear.

"I'd like to burn the fucking place," said Dave.

"No, just leave it as it is," the Lawyer replied. "These blokes are going to have a shock in a few hours time. My guess is that they'll be shitting themselves over where the stuff has gone. How the hell Vicki found out so quick I'd like to know? This stuff carries a pretty heavy prison sentence. I'd have thought they'd have it guarded. Where are we going to take it?"

"We dump it in the Medway," said Victor, "I ain't keeping hold of it, or at least not more than one night. We'll stick the vans in the other garage because it's starting to get light now and we ditch the stuff tomorrow night."

They all got into the vehicles which drove off. Except for Pete who was concentrating on his driving, all the other members of the Class were putting forward their own theories about who made up the child sex ring. Victor and the Lawyer, in separate vehicles both hit on the same ideas.

"I think this is how it goes," said the Lawyer to Charlie, "We're dealing with a major child sex ring. This is not your dirty mack brigade. These tapes are part of an import/export circle. They need to establish some legitimate outposts in Kent to move into the continent. They also need some outlets in the electronic side to provide cameras etc. for making more films, for copying and as a means of quickly distributing them. Video repairs you see. Simple. No more centralised mailing lists that can go missing. Just a series of cells of paedophiles who can go to their nearest pick-up point. If one point fails, if one cell is busted then the others carry on."

Charlie looked puzzled.

"Will people really go to this sort of length for this sort of stuff?"

"Yes. It's big business. It's also violent business. We are not just dealing with dodgy videos and a cushy prison sentence. If these bastards get caught do you know what's going to happen to them?"

"Long prison sentence?" guessed Charlie.

Charlie stopped at a red light and looked at the Lawyer.

"Sorry, I'm being as thick as Pete. I don't know."

"Well, child molesting is a worse crime in prison than murder. They will end up getting very badly done in by the other cons."

The van pulled away. The Lawyer continued.

"That's what I mean when I say this could get very nasty. There are currently several men who in the next few hours are going to find themselves desperate men, scared men. They will want to know where these videos have gone. They know it won't be the police because arrests would have followed immediately. They know it must be an organised operation because of the amount of videos lifted. So they are going to expect some sort of demand from whoever took the films, some sort of blackmail, because even without specific proof a rival firm could shop them to the police who would start asking some searching questions. If that doesn't come then they might put two and two together and come to the conclusion that either it's a rival paedophile network or another firm, namely us, out to bust them."

Charlie had by now started to race ahead with his thoughts.

"Which means we have to get Vicki out of that bloke's bedroom before they do put two and two together."

"She should be alright. She'll leave at dawn. She's not stupid. But this is what we are up against. I must admit I thought it might be drugs at first, just using videos as a side line, smuggling the stuff in through the video casing or something. But this is more dangerous."

"Yep. If it had been drugs they could almost let the thing go and shift the warehouse. But this is definitely heavy. This is definitely blackmail time. Do we blackmail? That would put the wind up them."

"We wait till we get back to Rochester, park the motors and go round to Victor's flat. This is going to need some thinking."

On reaching their second set of garages they parked the vehicles, locked the gates and congregated outside. Each mind was filled with thoughts about the ease in which they had carried out the night's work. They had expected some degree of trouble but none had come. As down-and-outs during a freezing night might break into a warm building seeking shelter, expecting authority to turf them out, so the Class had prepared for a guard at least. Now, like the tramp who had found a safe haven, they stood waiting for somebody to say something that would assure them that it really had been that easy. It was Victor's authoritative tones which broke the silence.

"Talk about stealing candy from a baby. I think we need to give some time to thinking about what we do next because the momentum is now definitely with us, and besides it's five in the morning and I don't know about other people but I'm tired. It might be the pain killers making me feel a bit drowsy but I'd like to get some sleep. Anyway, we have two options: one, we shop the bastards straight away to the police which would mean us having to explain why we engaged in breaking and entry, stealing and withholding information and would also expose our little operations. Or two, we dump the stuff and then contact them and tell them that either they get out of our territory or we blow everything to the cops. Get thinking. How about if we meet tonight about 7.00pm?"

Pete was examining the end of his baseball bat as if half disappointed that it had only been needed to bust open a box and grinned.

"OK, Victor, right on opening time," he said and then pondered why Rochester's pubs insisted on opening at this stupidly late hour.

"No, I think round our flat," answered Catherine, "Keep temptation away from Vic, no drinks you see."

With levelled eyes and a resigned look on his face Victor grunted something which sounded vaguely like "bloody doctors, bloody antibiotics."

"Good, that means I can get some sleep before opening my shop." said the Lawyer, "We still have legitimate businesses to run."

"Legitimate? You?" The Class gazed askance at the Lawyer.

"Well, alright, semi-legit... Well OK, OK... not really very legitimate at all, but it's still a business."

The Lawyer had succeeded in breaking the tense atmosphere, as a light shower of rain relieves a sticky humid night. They had so far achieved their objectives and a sense of relief washed over them. They bathed in this shower of comfort and dispersed contented.

Charlie and the Lawyer went off to their businesses, Louise and Dave went back to their home with Pete ambling beside, having been invited to stay and have breakfast, and Victor and Catherine went to their flat.

There was a message left on their answer phone for Catherine.

"Lovey, darling heart," said the familiar accentuated and extremely false accent.

"It's Lester," called Catherine to Victor who was making some toast.

"That director chap has found an absolutely suuuper new actress for you to work with. Found her yesterday. Quite divine dearest one. It would be quite wonderful if you could come up today and come on screen. Say about 4:00pm. I'll expect you darling. If you don't like the girl we'll just claim some more dosh off the film company for our extremely precise time. See you later."

"Hell," Catherine fell on the bed with her toast and then rested herself on her elbows like some ancient Roman at a feast, "that doesn't give much time. Listen Vic, I'll go up to London this afternoon. The shooting won't take more than a couple of hours and then I'll be back for the meeting."

The timing of the film set had slightly annoyed her coming as it did after a weekend that had had just too much excitement. But the film world was about seizing opportunities and being in the right place at the right time, of being the girl of the moment. Ever get a reputation for being unreliable and you would never be able to play the reluctant, pouting actress, you would never be able to play the Marilyn Monroe sulking in her dressing room. You'll be out. People underestimated the soft porn industry, it was as cut-throat as any other part of the film world. She knew of brilliant actresses who had been turned over because they had not been available and she had known others who had bedded their way to stardom. She fell back on the bed and fell asleep and started to have one of those restless dreams which were always intense and always forgotten on waking. Victor slumped in his throne, put his feet up on the coffee table and dropped off.

Louise and Dave had reached their small house quite quickly; it was only a short distance from garages. As their business was solely supplying and repairing they operated from one of the vans and had a more flexible system of hours. They were therefore not particularly tired as they sat down to breakfast. Both Dave and Louise were in their late twenties and had been part of the first generation of youngsters who had realised the future importance of computers and videos. Both had a respectable set of 'O' levels and had gone to comprehensive schools in London. They were also part of the last generation of young people who had benefited from a comprehensive education before the cut-backs which had started in the late seventies had slowly wrecked the system. Teachers had expected both of them to stay on and take 'A' levels and then do a conventional degree course at a higher education centre. But they had become fascinated by computers and while their contemporaries were studying Shakespeare or the development of the British political system they were immersed in an intense study of computer hardware. While their contemporaries were filling in UCCA forms and worrying about offers from universities they were developing programmes for computer games. They had gradually grown apart from their peers and rather as teenagers in a rock group might consider themselves an exclusive elite with a mission and a future so they developed their own life styles based on the knowledge that they were busting into new territories, opening up new ground for future generations. They became experts just at the time in the early eighties when computing technology was being recognised as being crucial. Before the market became flooded with computer and video wiz kids and before it had lost its pioneering phase, they had set up their own small and quite profitable business, working from home and creating their own network. Quite quickly they had realised that the new domain of computers was open to some creative usage and they therefore constantly delved into the criminal for a few jobs but always maintained a legitimate side to their affairs. As a couple they shied away from the conventional wisdom of the eighties. The idea of using their expertise for a company or for a steady income was not part of their life's philosophy. They were piratical and erratic in nature, sometimes working with an intensity which resembled the most committed scientist at their research and often going for days without doing anything more than servicing the regular customers. Had they not been so good they would have folded their business. Because both were excellent at their work they existed in a form of creative tension, a tension which sometimes exploded into arguments and would then invariably result in one of them walking out and not being seen for a few weeks. Their last violent row had involved a decision on whether or not to concentrate on free-lance work or whether one of them should try and get a temporary consultancy with a firm. The row had reached violent proportions and had ended with Dave coming close to hitting Louise, but instead he had picked up a vase and smashed it over his own head in frustration. He had walked out and gone to the local hospital for some stitches to his skull and had then booked into a hotel in Cornwall for a week. A few days ago he had come back to find that, as always, the incident had been forgotten and the issue which caused it in the first place had been resolved. At the moment they were contented and were working together again quite happily. They sat down on the floor with their cups of tea whilst Pete sat in a corner with a sausage sandwich enveloped in his giant-like hands trying unsuccessfully to stop the fat from dripping down his shirt. He beamed across his face and said something to the effect that a visit to the launderette would soon be in order. Louise produced from her bag a couple of the videos they had lifted from the warehouse.

"I've never seen a sicko film before. Thought I'd take a couple. We can destroy them afterwards."

She placed the cassette into the machine and pressed the play button. The title came on, 'A School Girl's Playtime.' The quality of the recording was not particularly good but the images on the screen were horrific.

A young girl, who could not have been more than ten was standing up against a bedroom wall. She whispered in a hesitant and choking voice,

"I want to play."

Grasping the hem of her skirt with both hands she slowly raised it above the knee and then slowly up her thighs until it revealed her knickers. She lifted the hem of the skirt right up to her chin and pushed her hips forwards and backwards in a gentle thrusting motion.

"Does anyone want to play with me?" she mumbled. A nude male walked onto the screen and stood next to her, slipping one of his hands into her blouse he masturbated with the other. He wore a mask to hide his face but she looked straight at the camera lens. To look at the lower half of her face was to see a mouth forced into a half smile, to look at the upper half was to see eyes which pleaded for an end. To see the face as a whole was to see a child in torment. The man whispered into the child's ear. It must have been something to do with looking cheerful for the smile widened although the eyes went into a deeper terror. The man had released her hands from their grip and the skirt flopped back into position until he undid the clasp and started to pull it down. Her eyes stared into lens as if begging the viewer for mercy and pity. The camera moved down her body and went into a close-up as the man started to remove her knickers. Louise and Dave and Pete looked at the screen and they saw before them the death agony of a Nazi concentration camp victim and the torture of a South African black in a police cell. They watched as if on this screen were all the countless horrors that had ever been inflicted on the world's helpless. The shock of witnessing the perverting of innocence was too much for Pete who started to weep. Louise flicked the off-button.

"Fucking hell. Those bastards are going to fucking die."

Pete's large frame was quivering as he started to cry openly.

"Why do they do this sort of thing?" he asked. "She's too young, too young."

He rubbed both hands furiously across his face removing the tears and sat brooding revenge.

"They're perverts alright," said Dave. "And now I see why they want in on our side of the operation. The quality of that film was poor. They want high tech equipment to really clean up. They are also going to need some decent copying machines for a fast distribution network."

"If by now those evil people have discovered that their store had been raided then I think there are a few worried perverts around at the moment."

"There will be a few dead perverts pretty soon!" added Pete.

Chapter 16

Charlie went to his home and got a couple of restless hours sleep. His dreams whirled inside his subconscious: children with baseball bats; film makers; public school types and enormous warehouses spun round and round. He awoke at 8:00am not really refreshed from the sleep. As often when a tired mind awakes thoughts became intense and concentrated. While he showered ideas thundered through him, the adrenaline rose causing him to scrub furiously, splashing his shower foam over the bathroom floor. He had that same nervous anticipation which he had felt back in '79 during the health service low pay strikes of that year.

That was the year when he had been first elected as district secretary for his union, a step up from being a shop steward. He had felt an awesome responsibility during that strike of wrestling with the moral implications of taking industrial action within the health service. During that dispute he had felt for the first time what it was like to stand outside the norms of society and not to take for granted what the papers, the government and educated opinion had told him. The experience was the single most important influence on his life and the feeling he experienced during the low pay strikes never left him. It was a feeling of anger and determination and a feeling of strength and commitment. It was also a belief that what they were doing was right, morally right and politically right. He had formed a set of beliefs from that experience which fitted in nicely with the general beliefs of the Class; he liked working with people from different businesses and had the same business ethics as the rest, based on a dodgy and semi-illegal code of practice. He had used his energy and his negotiating skills to set up his car firm after he had been sacked from his job as a hospital porter. The actual reasons for his dismissal were becoming blurred but it was all part of the government shake out of union activists in the NHS in the early eighties. Suffice it to say that the union had called it a blatant case of victimisation and since his dismissal the union had been effectively broken in his hospital and the management had been allowed to make the cuts that they wanted.

Since then he had gradually developed his business and had now started to deal in old models which were becoming in demand. The other day he had actually sold an old Anglia deluxe from the sixties for an inflated price. What he was going to get for his new intake of fifties cars he didn't know, but things were starting to look up, providing that the police did not sniff too carefully around his operation.

He finished showering and got dressed, eating a quick breakfast; he was down in his showroom as his assistant was opening up. Custom was always slow during August as most car buyers used their cash to get hold of one of the new registration rather than a second hand model. At 9.15am he was inspecting a new second hand acquisition, wondering whether he should re-spray it when a questioning voice made him turn round.

"Good morning Charlie."

"Hello Sergeant Campbell. Nothing illegal going on here you know."

The lie didn't sound convincing, nor was it meant to be. The police would bust him if they could really pin anything on him.

"We know that. How is Rochester's very own Arthur Daley?"

"Making a living, when I'm not being disturbed. However, as you know officer I'm always ready to help our boys in blue."

That sentence sounded even less convincing than the first but it was all part of the game.

"This is Inspector Benjamin. He'd like to ask you some questions."

Campbell turned to his boss and said in a tone which was meant to suggest that they hadn't already talked about Charlie before coming to his showroom.

"Charlie here used to be a shop steward, but now he's joined the capitalist class."

"Nothing wrong with being a shop steward," said Benjamin, "my father was one on the print, although they used to call themselves fathers of chapels instead of shop stewards."

Charlie wanted to say something like 'don't patronise me' but instead he kept up the game.

"Well gents, shall we go into my office for a cup of tea?"

They stepped into his back office which was small but tidy and well ordered, complete with a small regiment of filing cabinets. Charlie made the tea whilst they exchanged pleasantries about cricket, the weather and whether the modern design of the Rolls-Royce was superior to the old design. The situation was so cliché riddled that when the cups were handed out Charlie felt the game should be taken onto its next stage.

"Well I know you busy police officers have not come down at this hour to talk about the state of the England cricket team, so what's up?"

Inspector Benjamin took a sip from his tea and began yet another set of questioning which he hoped would be more fruitful and revealing than Victor's. He soon realised why Charlie was once a shop steward, his faced had assumed a poker like expression giving nothing away.

"You saw Victor over the weekend?"

"Yes, Saturday lunch time. I think you had talked to him before we arrived."

"Then you should know about our concern with a child sex ring and possible illegal videos."

It was quite obvious to Charlie that they were attempting to get him to talk about Victor's activities, but he thought he might as well do some question asking himself. He was in the mood for some negotiating and probing, he'd treat these police officers just as he'd treated the management at his hospital.

"I don't understand what you're getting at. Victor ain't the one for those sort of films, you should know that. Anyway, I don't know how a child porno network operates."

"Actually Charlie, you have hit on the right phrase for describing these people. We do believe that it is a network of some rather nasty people who are clever enough to cover their tracks. They seem to be moving in on your group's territory, what do you call yourself, the Class, strange name?"

"We are called the Class because we are classy and because we act as a class. I think it's called a metaphor."

"You think correctly. A metaphor it is, but your metaphor is under a bit of pressure at the moment, you have heard of the beating given out to Dave, Victor and the other chap."

Charlie didn't fall into the trap.

"I thought Victor was mugged. Dave was the one who was beaten up."

"Well quite. We just wanted to warn you to be careful."

"Thanks, but I really can't see what a child molesters' network would want with me. I really don't understand how they work."

"Well, I'll explain so that you know. Because of the nature of their crime and the public approbation which goes with it, child pornography is very secretive. It is also very big money especially if, as we think is correct this gang is supplying videos and possibly live sex shows to some pillars of the community. They are going to defend themselves as best they can and that means violently. However, we think that they may have over reached themselves. We think that drugs are now involved and this attempt to diversify might just break them. They are relying on the relaxation of custom laws between us and Europe to get the stuff through. It's just that in order to corner the European market they may have moved too soon. So at the moment they may be vulnerable. Therefore if they do try and put any pressure on any member of your group, yourself included, then come and contact me.

"You see, we think that the people who attacked Dave and...errrr... perhaps Victor and his friend are part of this set-up."

He paused waiting for any change in Charlie's visage, but his expression remained studiously blank.

"Thanks for the warning," said Charlie as they got up to leave.

"Oh yes, and one other thing," Benjamin was going to play his final ace, "if you hear of anything on the pub grapevine about where these crooks may be operating from, let us know. The landlord would have nothing to lose in cooperating with us."

At the back of Charlie's eye a faint glow appeared, Benjamin noticed it but said nothing:

"Thanks for the tea, back to the station, sergeant."

They left Charlie in his office.

"Why the mention of the landlord?" asked Campbell as they climbed into their car.

"Because he knows where the criminals hang out, he's been there. I saw it, the one flicker in his eyes, I saw it. Take this car round the corner and wait and see if Charlie makes any move."

Back in his office Charlie made ready to go to London unaware that he was being watched. As this was the slack time of year he could just leave a list for his assistant: three cars to be cleaned out and a couple of small repairs for a friend. He got into his car, turned out of the drive and started on the road to the Medway Bridge. Behind him Benjamin and Campbell were following. They had already phoned through the licence plate for other cars to take up the lead if they lost him or if they thought he was aware that they were following. The chances were that they would have to lose him just before London, that would be the most convenient place.

"If he is going to London," remarked Campbell.

"Bound to be. And if not, well we start again. Who knows we may even get some time to look into those break-ins in Strood."

They were not to be disappointed. Charlie was unaware that he was being followed and was heading towards the Grapes.

"Hello," said Benjamin, "Southwark. Scene of many a murky deal."

"Sixties gangsters and all that," replied Campbell.

At the Walworth Rd. they decided to leave their quarry as he turned into a side road and Campbell could just see that he had stopped. They would take the next road and come up on him. Charlie had indeed stopped a few yards away from the Grapes. He paused for a few moments staring ahead of him. Something was not quite right, his shop steward's instincts which had served him well to warn him of impending trouble were now registering a high level on the danger scale. The pub looked the same, the bunting still hung limply like the faded relic that it was, the curtains remained half opened giving the impression of the pub being either permanently open or permanently closed and the posters in the window were still there advertising live music on Friday and Saturday nights with a smaller notice saying strip tease each Sunday and Wednesday lunch times. Yet something was wrong. Charlie slowly got out of his car and walked hesitatingly towards the door, his hands in his pockets, his eyes fixed on the door. And then he realised what it was. The door was shut, this pub like most other pubs during the summer months would have its doors open at lunch time. There was also something else wrong: there were too many cars parked outside, like so many guests' cars at a wedding trying to get into a limited parking space. He stopped in the middle of the road and looked at the building. At that moment the door flung open and a person came spilling onto the pavement, almost losing his balance he shouted frantically at Charlie,

"Run, run, get out of here fast."

It was John Wilson who was shouting and he tore at Charlie grabbing him by the arm and steering him away down the road. For a moment Charlie resisted the movement but it was only momentarily for out of the pub poured five or six men with violence in their eyes. Charlie started to turn and to follow the charging John but his initial inertia allowed the leading men to catch him and Charlie felt a knife slash across his cheek. He spun on his heels and thundered a fist into the man's jaw sending him reeling backwards against one of the parked cars. With that Charlie took off and raced down the road following John. The men were following fast and they were gaining on Charlie. A car crept round the corner a few feet in front of him and he clumsily vaulted over the bonnet to escape collision, knocking one of the windscreen wipers out of its position as he did so. The driver pressed down on his brakes and the car halted effectively blocking pursuit. As one of the hunters tried to follow Charlie over the bonnet the passenger threw open the door and caught him heavily on his right shoulder, felling the man to the ground.

"Police, hold it right there you lot."

Benjamin dragged the fallen man to his feet as Campbell came round from the other side.

"Right, you lot up against the wall."

One of the men was half flung against the wall when another cried out,

"It's those two you want. They tried to steal our car."

Had Benjamin not known that the fleeing man was Charlie he would have believed him. As it was he knew that this was a bare lie.

"I see a man trying to steal a car against five men armed with flick knives. Pull the other one matey."

One of the men looked as if he was about to run but Campbell had pulled out his gun and aimed it right at him.

"Don't even consider it chum. Now, considering that flick knives are strictly illegal and seeing as some bodily harm has been done to the fleeing gentleman, whether he had perpetrated some crime against you or not I think we have sufficient grounds for pulling you lot in."

Benjamin called for assistance on his radio and within a couple of minutes the men were being taken away for questioning. Benjamin was completely sure that these five characters were the first major step in busting the child porn ring and he was starting to feel pleased with himself.

Charlie had continued running and had only looked behind him once to see the car prevent further chase. He thought the men pursuing him would have been frightened by the idea of a witness identifying them. He did not realise that the police were now firmly involved.

John was waiting for him around a corner and put out his hand to stop him, bringing him to a sudden halt he breathed,

"We'll have to get out of here. Can you make it to that phone box over there, I can get help?"

They walked quickly to the box, the blood was starting to run down Charlie's shirt, it was warm on his hand and the cut did not hurt but the shock did. He was momentarily stunned like an animal that had been trapped before the kill. He felt mesmerised by the idea that he had been cut and was not thinking clearly, crashing into the box he swore and tried to regain composure.

"Don't worry, you're in a state of shock," said John as he phoned a friend. "A couple of minutes and we'll get you to a safe house, nobody will know where we are."

He looked at the cut,

"On second thoughts, I think we ought to get you to a hospital, that's going to need stitches."

Charlie leaned up against a wall and searched for a handkerchief, he was almost faint on seeing so much of his own blood.

"And me feeling sick at the sight of blood after years of working in the health service. Listen, I guessed who you are, you're John. I'm Charlie, one of Victor's friends."

He was dabbing at the wound as the blood congealed. John supported him,

"Yes I know you are and you almost walked right into it there. But here's the car I'll tell you what happened."

John's girlfriend was driving and she said a few words of comfort as the car sped off to the nearest casualty. John started to explain.

"Your lot have really done it now. I've never seen Nigel Croft-White and his mob so wild. The landlord just shut the door and wouldn't let anyone in or out. What did you do?"

"We busted their warehouse and nicked their videos, kiddy porn amongst the films."

"That's why they were so up tight. They blamed me at first and I was bloody scared. You was recognised by one of the old dears who was looking out of the window. She shouted out that you was with the stripper on Sunday, when there had been trouble. Something a half pissed old woman might call out but nobody added things up until Croft-White said something about 'Sharon' and he started talking rapidly to his mate Dominic."

"I know what he had worked out. You see Sharon is really our Vicki and she was the one who tipped us off."

"That makes sense, so while they were talking I got my chance. This bloke wasn't really paying much attention to me so I dived out the door and the rest you know, painfully."

"Bloody good job you did, thanks."

They had arrived at the hospital casualty and Charlie reported to the desk to be met by the comment.

"A knife fight, and it's only Monday lunchtime. What is South London coming to?"

'Reception porters haven't lost their sense of wit I see,' thought Charlie as he sat down and waited. The familiar sights and atmosphere of a hospital casualty reassured him; the clinical smell, the nurses rushing about, the G and E size air cylinders stacked in a corner and the green gowned theatre porters pushing trolleys. His trained eye noticed that student nurses were carrying out the duties of a nursing auxiliary and that there were too few porters for a casualty of this size and that there was a distinct absence of cleaning staff.

'The cuts must have gone deeper than we expected,' he thought and then admired the pun that he had just made by grinning and touching his own deep cut.

"Well, at least you can still smile," said John.

At the Grapes Nigel Croft-White was furious. He felt that for once events were slipping from beyond him. A rage developed within him, it burned inside his brain, he believed it was shaking his head in a violent but enclosed vibration. People around him experienced the terror of association with a mind which was seething with rage. Nobody dared to speak. Within a few moments they became aware that for the first time Croft-White had lost and he himself was conscious of the failure. Seb Austen and Dominic Davidson felt that something was wrong, they were on the verge of understanding what it was like to be a victim, to be a failure in a life style where success breeds power and where anything other than success ultimately creates a gap through which will follow a collapse. For once they felt isolated, but only for a moment for Croft-White acted swiftly.

"Right, five of our lot are in police hands, they won't talk and the police can't prove anything. We leave fast and if any of you lot identify any of us as being part of any act of violence I will personally cut all of you to ribbons."

He spoke to the landlord, the old lady and two of the regulars who were the only customers. He spoke with the accents of terror knowing full well that any weakness at this time would be fatal. The remaining members of his mob got into their cars and drove to their warehouse where an immediate conference was held. Croft-White had worked out the next moves.

"Right, Seb, what was the name of that drugged up tart that you got a job in a porno film for?"

"Jenny."

"Do you remember where she said she'd been turned down by an agent?"

"Yeah, it was that one just by London Bridge. Hammer went with her to the film studio didn't you?"

Hammer nodded in affirmation.

"OK Hammer, you know you said that she went berserk when she saw the agent who had turned her down coming onto the set with the other girl, yeah, well what was that girl's other name?"

"Catherine," said Hammer, who then quickly added, "and she looked just like the girl who started to strip in the pub the other day."

"She was the same fucking girl," said Croft-White who was now beginning to re-assume control over events as he realised who had stolen the videos. He felt a purpose and a direction had come back to him and like a general who had just received reinforcements he worked out his plan quickly and communicated it to his force,

"I thought that was the case. It makes sense now. Seb and Dom go to the agent's office and lean on him pretty heavily. Get him to phone her to come to the office and when she comes take her. If she comes with her mate Sharon, or whatever her name is, get her instead. We'll do a swap, their Sharon for our tapes."

The mob felt happy with this, they united once more around their boss.

"And whilst you lot are doing that I think me and a couple others are going to pay a little visit to wanker Wilson's shop and see if he's around. I'll just call our friends down at the Travellers' camp, we may need some more muscle." He picked up a wall phone, dialled and spoke rapidly before placing it back and saying, "That's OK, let's go."

They left the buildings and swept away. In fact Croft-White was too late to catch Arthur for a warning phone call from his son had sent him running for his car keys and within a minute he was on the move towards the safety of John's girlfriend's house. Once again something had gone wrong for Croft-White, he had failed to anticipate events and whilst he didn't show it, he felt a sense that events might just be moving against him. The exchange of the videos for the girl would save them, but he'd have to ensure that there was sufficient pressure on Manning and his mob not to go to the police. He felt the exhilaration of danger, just as he had experienced it quite a few years ago when he had once been cornered by a rival mob, cornered in a quiet and dark back street. It had been then that he had used his brains and his fists to turn the trap on his pursuers. They had fought without rules, without any pity and without any mercy and their rivals had been sent sprawling away, blood covering their clothes. And now he believed he was experiencing the same sensations, he was like an enclosed case of energy waiting to explode.

Chapter 17

At 2.00pm Catherine was woken by the ringing of their front door bell. It was Vicki.

"How did it go last night, everyone fine, how's Pete?"

Her voice was anxious but still in control.

"Don't worry, everyone and everything is just great and Pete's having breakfast round Louise and Dave's," replied Catherine. "Go and wake Victor will you whilst I get some coffee. Then you can tell us what happened last night. After that I've got to go up to London this afternoon. Fancy driving me there? I think Pete's a bit worn out after last night?"

Victor jolted awake at the sound of Vicki's voice. He was still tired and extremely stiff from sleeping in the chair and from the injuries he had sustained. In fact he got up from his throne like a man four times his age might, but he didn't show it to Vicki who had dropped onto the settee and spread herself out like Mata Hari at her most persuasive. Catherine came in with the cups and Victor's pills and then Vicki started.

"You are not going to believe this," she commenced deliberately creating suspense.

"Coming from you Vicki nothing would surprise me," grinned Victor. "However, from your cheeky and very smug smirk I take it the posh bastard didn't have his wicked way with you."

"Are you joking or something. It was easy. These thugs don't know what they are up against with us. Nigel Croft-White, that's the bloke's name Victor, didn't twig at all who we were. He thought I was just some tart or something. And I'll hit either of you who quip that that's exactly what I am."

"Wouldn't dream of it," said Victor.

"So this is what happened. We went to this Italian restaurant up near Tottenham Court Rd. and had something to eat. Nigel is real public school you know. He got thrown out of one for drugs and got himself accepted into a more minor one. That apparently is what they do you know, throw their rejects from one school to another. He told me that after school he had met these other public school kiddies and they were squatting in some vacant council property in Camden. Any roads, this property had just been done up for a local family to move into, man wife and two kids and these public school wallies claimed squatters' rights. They refused to leave unless the council found them other accommodation. It got really heated and got onto the local news."

"I remember that," said Catherine. "We talked about it at school. Wasn't there something heavy about it or something."

"Yes. You see it turns out that the property had been specially fitted with a new bathroom because one of the children was severely disabled and they had ramps fitted out into the back garden etc. The young family turned up at the house complete with a film crew and begged these squatters to leave. Of course they refused and the camera really picked up their public school accents and the press went mad over it. What got me is that when Nigel Croft-White was telling me all this he did so in such a matter of fact way as if it was all the council's fault. The local residents were apparently up in arms in case the council allowed these posh blokes to jump the queue, ahead of local people. They still refused to move and one night it happened."

"What, the council brought in the police?" asked Victor.

"No, all this was before the changes in the property laws. Remember they are about ten years older than us. No, what happened was that a whole bunch of local heavies went into the house and flung them out and really done them over and told them that if they tried to get back in they'd be dead. They moved the family in there and then."

"Bloody good job and all," said Victor. "Anyway how does this interesting story fit in with our situation?"

"Oh, it set up their attitude as a group. They started to work together so he told me. He got quite arrogant about what they were involved with although I think that most of it was lies. It was almost as if he had a need to boast about the whole thing. You know, Catherine, the usual macho thing of impressing the girlfriend with tales of past achievements."

Catherine nodded in agreement and looked playfully at Victor who spat out in amazement,

"I bloody well don't bloody boast about my bloody past achievements."

"No, I know you don't lover but you don't half rise to the bait sometimes."

"Have you noticed how Victor swears a lot when he's sober?" said Vicki. "You need a drink to wash your mouth out with."

She knew full well that this was not possible but at the moment she was feeling pleased with her achievement of the night before like a student gaining a grade A for a difficult piece of work.

"Sorry Victor, I'll get on with it. Any roads they are into videos and video machines and cameras, lighting and all that stuff. He told me that they were making films and even asked me if I wanted to appear in one. God he was oily, just like that Spitting Image puppet of that Tory politician, you know the one they make up as a slug?"

"Parkinson, the sex pot," said Catherine.

"No, it's Baker," said Victor.

"Doesn't matter, they're all the same."

"So we finished our meal which I've got to hand it to him he did know how to choose the right course on the menu and we goes for a drive in his Roller to this small basement and watched these orientals doing a most amazing play or dance thing. They were using swords and knives and things. I couldn't make it out but some of the moves were flipping erotic; almost as good as you, Cathy. Any roads he sort of keeps introducing me to people, you know the usual male thing of letting everyone know that he's got himself a pretty girly, status symbol and all that."

She paused and glanced challengingly at Victor who frowned at her and gave the two fingered 'fuck off' sign as if to say 'I'm not responding to that one get on with it.' She drew her breath and continued,

"To carry on with the story, he gets us something else to eat and by now it's getting late so he obviously thinks to himself that as he's shown me a good time and as I'm suitably impressed that I'd allow him to take me to his flat for a bit of a grope. So he asks me and I says I don't mind going home with him to his flat which is in the posh part of Islington. So we gets there and very yuppie it is too. He starts to get all romantic and sloppy but it was not the usual guff, there was something wrong. I mean it was almost completely clichéd and corny, like he was doing this for show or something."

"I'll tell you why it was wrong."

Victor sat back down in his throne and leant forward on the long wooden arms.

"It's because they are all perverts, into child porn and all that."

Vicki's eyes widened in recognition like a detective who had just found the final clue to a difficult case.

"Oh it fits now, I thought he wasn't just kinky. You see I told him I was a tart and would only do it for £30. And he said that he wanted something special, he wanted me to dress up."

"Don't tell me," groaned Victor who had guessed what was coming, "as a girl guide."

"Nope," said Vicki, "but you're close."

"As a schoolgirl?" hazarded Catherine.

"Yep, complete with spanking."

"Fuck me!" said Catherine.

"No thanks. Any roads I digress so I'll finish this off. I asked to see his money and he puts it on the mantle piece and said if I was an extra naughty girl..."

Vicki was mimicking and accentuating the public school accent and had pulled her knees together with her hands between them acting out the standard 'sweet and innocent pose',

"...he'd give me an extra ten quid. So I played along with him and started to say that I'd been a very naughty girl at school and deserved to be punished, whilst he got out the uniform. And it was there you know, the whole bloody lot complete with navy blue knickers. So I told him to take a shower whilst I got changed and the wally did. Whilst he was doing that I looked in his diary and saw that they had just moved a whole load of videos from an address that I couldn't make out although it was definitely foreign to the one I gave you and that they were going to move them the next night to several addresses throughout the home counties. That was when I phoned you."

Victor was pleased with this account it answered a major question.

"That was why the warehouse was quite easy to break into for us. It was only a temporary one, to keep the stuff in transit."

Catherine wanted the analysis later, she wanted to hear the end.

"Come on, what happened. He didn't do anything, or so you say."

"No he flipping well didn't because I didn't let him. Whilst he was happily having a shower I took the money and skipped out, got a cab and caught the last train back from Charing Cross."

On mentioning this she abruptly changed the subject.

"And talking of which do you know that they don't have any loos on those trains and that blokes who've had a skinful piss out of the window. The drunks' express I call it. And this bloke was sick, the vomit comet it ought to be called. Disgusting."

"If a man's got to go then a man's got to go!" judge Victor pronounced. "It's British Rail's fault."

He once again rose creakily from his seat, went across to Vicki and gave her a little kiss on the cheek saying as he did so,

"Bloody good work there Vicki. Bloody good. But what I'd like to know is why did you nick the money? It could have had him coming after you. He might have thrown a dressing gown on and chased you like a thief or something."

Catherine put up her hand to interrupt him and added,

"No, that was a master stroke. Friend Croft-wanker is going to think that Vicki really is a prostitute. Had she not taken the money he might have started to think a bit and perhaps started to suspect something. No, he probably just spent the night thinking that he'd been ripped off. Brilliant thinking."

Vicki took a bow and placed her hands on imaginary lapels before answering,

"Elementary my dear Catherine."

Catherine got up and walked towards the bathroom.

"I've got to get ready before going up to London, so I'll just take a shower first. Do you want to drive me up there Vicki or are you tired?"

"I'll drive you. I'm never tired."

Catherine busied herself in the shower singing to herself whilst Victor and Vicki chatted over another cup of coffee. Vicki questioned Victor in depth over last night's activities and then asked,

"What I don't understand is why do they need to take over every dealer you supply to and why take over every aspect of Louise and Dave's electronics?"

"Oh that's fairly straight forward. What would you think if a firm came up to you, threatened you and said they wanted only part of your business."

"I'd start to ask questions, like why do they only want to takeover only part of the business." Vicki emphasised each of the words like a student who had realised that she's asked a rather obvious question.

"Quite." Victor paused over his coffee and looked at the clock and smiled to himself.

"What's up?" asked Vicki.

"Well, I should think by now friend Croft-wanker will have found out that his tapes are gone and will be feeling pretty sick. My guess is that their firm will be meeting and trying to work out who did it. Bloody hell, there are going to be some recriminations in that firm."

"Yep. He will probably have his bottom spanked for this."

"Actually it is more likely that he'll try and shift the blame onto somebody else in the organisation. It almost makes these bloody bruises and the bloody lack of beer worthwhile, but not quite. We haven't finished yet with this lot. We'll discuss tonight how we proceed, personally I'd like to keep the police out of it and really put the frighteners on them, but we certainly haven't finished with them yet, not by a long shot."

Chapter 18

Within half an hour Vicki was speeding Catherine towards London in her car. To say 'speeding' was to talk in a literal sense for Vicki rarely kept within the limit. Her driving was also wildly eccentric, treating as she did every other driver on the road as a rival. Catherine had forgotten just how erratic her driving was and she sat staring in disbelief as Vicki somehow managed to jump in between two vehicles and cross over into another lane without hitting a cyclist in the process. Catherine breathed in heavily and commented,

"I bet when you were a kid bumper cars were your favourite fun fair attraction."

"Yep," replied Vicki who on seeing a pedestrian let out an almighty Banshee-like scream,

"Eeeeeeeeeeeeeeehhh."

The pedestrian jumped and looked round at the oncoming Vicki who was glaring at him, threatening him to try and cross.

"Bastard!" she added at the top of her voice.

"Ummm, Vicki dear, I do think that the pedestrian had a right to cross there, it was after all a Zebra crossing."

"I know but then you see I'm just a mental case."

"Quite."

"Which is why I like Pete."

"Quite."

"Any roads, I'll slow down now, don't want to get stopped before we get to London, do we? Can I stay and watch the filming. I've never seen a porno film in the making."

"Only if you promise to keep within the speed limit there and back," said a relieved Catherine as the speedometer went below fifty for the first time. "Actually there's nothing really much to see. We've got this lesbian scene to do. It won't take long, it might not even happen if the other actress is as moronic as the drugged up suicide case I had to deal with on Saturday."

"You like your work don't you?" grinned Vicki.

"Yes, it makes a living, a very good one at that. So long as you keep your wits about you and keep every situation well under control."

"OK then, if I may ask a question which I've been longing to ask ever since I found out about your politics; how can you square your job with your support for the loony right wing politicians and all that crap? I mean they are supposed to support Victorian values, you know morality and everything. I can't see Maggie T going to a strip show or approving of porno videos."

"I don't support their policies or their Party, I just like their attitudes. They don't whinge, they act. They don't give in, they fight. They ain't weak and wimpish like the new style Labourites. I mean for all his rugby playing stuff Kinnock was still only good at fighting those he didn't like in the Labour Party. He was good at bashing the left but not good at bashing the Tories. I mean Tebbit kicked his way to the top, didn't he? Before the Labour Party went soft blokes like him would have been Socialists, like that fat bastard from Liverpool who died a couple of years back, Heffer. I liked him and I like Prescott and Skinner but the rest are wimps."

"'Cor, macho feminist!" Vicki exclaimed.

"I'm not a feminist. Feminists are all middle class girlies who don't give a damn about working class women. Feminism is about replacing a bunch of middle class male drips with a bunch of middle class female drips."

From the harsh tones she employed and the strident attitude of 'no compromise' Vicki could see why Catherine got on so well with Victor. They were both similar in their desperate approach life. Vicki asked another question.

"OK, then why are you against kiddi porn? Where do you draw a line at the age? 14 years old, or 16 or 18? Where does childhood end and adulthood begin?"

"I'd say at 18 and anyway come off it Vicki, child porn is different. Most of them are forced into it by sick parents. You know that from your own background."

Vicki nodded in acknowledgement. However, she asked another,

"Right, I accept that the girls have to be a certain age and be in full awareness of what they are doing. But what about the perverts who get off on schoolgirl stuff, Nigel and his posh bastards?"

"I'd never do that kind of pose or any film that sees underage girls as being sex objects. That is sick. Any other questions deary?"

"You were starting to sound almost as sarcastic as me then, but I have to agree with you about your job but not about your attitude to life. I mean to say don't you think that people are getting a bit fed up with that kind of aggressive gutsy right-wing political approach," she explained. "I mean Maggie has gone and a new lot are taking over. I think that a caring approach is needed, people have suffered a great deal and they are worried about the health service and education. The quality of life is important you know. Any roads, I'm a Labour supporter, except I do wish they'd stop rabbiting on all the time. They're as bad as me, real chatter boxes."

Their conversation had taken them to the outskirts of London now and Vicki was starting to drive more carefully, trying to work out where the studio was. Catherine directed her from London Bridge Station and they were soon inside the building.

As before the camera crew were getting the set ready, crossing cables and hooking them up with a dexterity which told of years of practice. Jim the director and Lester saw them come in and waved a cheerful greeting like two adolescent schoolboys who had just seen their first date walking through the door having spent the last half hour anxiously wondering if they were going to be stood up.

"How great to see you again," said Jim. "Look I really am sorry about Saturday. The poor girl was washed out on drugs and her agent was really her pimp. Sorry, I didn't know. The new actress is in the changing room and she's good, very good."

"I'm relieved to hear it," replied Catherine winking at Lester. "I don't think you two have ever met my friend Vicki. She drove me here and she wants to stay and watch."

Lester was up to his usual pretentious standards when he exclaimed,

"Lovey, darling, what a superb friend you have. I say, lovey Vicki have you ever considered going into movies. I could make you a star. Have you ever wanted your name in bright lights? You'd be huge."

He emphasised his words by throwing his arms in the air and waving them about. Vicki found Lester hilarious and hid her face in her chest giggling and shaking her head.

"No she doesn't Lester, so leave her alone," interjected Catherine.

"Quite right Cathy," said Jim who wanted to get on with the filming.

He walked Catherine over to the dressing room door.

"Thanks for coming up on time. I really thought we'd blown it with you after last Saturday and the budget is tight on this one."

Jim was gentle for a director and had none of the ruthlessness which often went with the job. He looked after the good actresses and the good camera crews and because of this had kept the company going whilst other film businesses went to the wall during the recession; and in the process he had gained a reputation for shooting quality films. Catherine appreciated being treated decently and she enjoyed working with him.

"Right, introduce us," she said as she opened the dressing room door.

"Alex, this is Cathy. Cathy, Alex, who by the state of undress is already to start. Don't forget to put your dressing gown on and come onto the set looking tired. Right, I'll leave you to get ready."

Catherine smiled at the new face.

"I haven't seen you on the circuit. Are you new to this line of business?"

"No, just to this part of the country. I've been operating up North, dancing mainly, at working mens clubs and places like that."

It was a friendly voice which answered Catherine and was accompanied by a friendly smile.

"But I've heard of you and seen a couple of your films. I thought they were very good, particularly 'A Southern Affair.' Very erotic. I think you've got a gorgeous body."

Alex was watching Catherine undress with a studious gaze.

"I like your breasts," she continued whilst looking down at her own, "mine are too small."

Alex rose from her chair and moved around the room picking up objects and examining them in an idle and time passing manner. She was in her late teens or early twenties and her lightly tanned figure was small but well proportioned and had a fine muscle tone suggesting regular exercise and training. Her short cut hair had been dyed peroxide blonde and contrasted with the natural dark colouring of her pubic hair. When she moved she did so with quick darting movements which gave the impression of an active and assertive character. She leaned forward over the dressing table and started to toy with a small hand mirror. Her motions reminded Catherine of an athlete or of a classically educated dancer for they had a certain ease to them. When she stood still she had a poise and elegance with head erect as if she had just completed an exercise in graceful movement. With both hands on her hips and her legs slightly apart she exuded confidence and ability. She also had a calmness about her which pleased Catherine who had by now summed up her fellow actress and had come to the conclusion that she had real class.

"Tell me if I'm being nosy but you look as if you've had some sort of training in movement and dance."

"Oh, not anything after my school. We did dance there and had elocution lessons and training in how to be a lady," said Alex who was looking intently at Catherine's naked body and was breathing gently but audibly. Standing still and slightly swaying from side to side she clasped her hands behind her back and looked fully and coyly into Catherine's eyes.

"Gosh, but you are gorgeous."

She moved towards Catherine with lips parted in an expectant smile, her tongue slightly protruding and moistening the top lip.

"Hang on a minute," Catherine winced at the advance and took a step back, "you're not a bloody..."

She was interrupted by a precise if sultry reply.

"I am a disciple of Sappho from the Island of Lesbos!" broke in Alex.

"A fucking what from fucking where?" shouted Catherine.

"A lesbian," retorted Alex smiling.

"Fuck me," yelled Catherine.

"That is what I am being paid to do and on film too."

"No you fucking well ain't. Fucking hell, first I get a fucking drugged crazed fucking tart and then I get a fucking dyke."

Catherine had turned her back on Alex and had buried her face in her hands swearing through her fingers. Alex waited a few moments before speaking.

"Why don't we do it, Catherine. I mean you have to admit that I'm pretty good. I could see you sizing me up right from the start. I bet you came to the conclusion right away that you could do this scene with me. You see, apart from the way I am I'm also a professional and so are you and us professionals really must keep the erotic going. Yes, darling, I know about your attitude towards declining standards and I quite agree with them. So with me getting turned on during this scene by your quite incredible body it won't be acting on my part it will be real and therefore will be a masterpiece of eroticism. So how about it? How about acting like a real professional?"

The logic was remorseless and she had hit on Catherine's pride in her job. Catherine had no real choice, she could not really expect Jim to delay for a second time because her partner was bent and even if she did who would replace Alex? Another junky, another clapped out whore?

"Oh well," she sighed, "let's get on with it."

Alex threw her arm around Catherine's shoulder and gave Catherine a squeeze,

"Brilliant lover," she said, "let's knock them dead."

Alex opened the door and marched playfully arm in arm with Catherine onto the set smiling at everybody. Catherine looked resignedly at Vicki and mouthed the word 'butch'. Vicki burst out laughing and explained what Catherine had said to Lester who dropped his lower jaw and went wide eyed. He started to sing the words of 'It must be love' to a mildly fed up Catherine who by now was standing by the bed, frowning with both hands folded over her chest. She did not feel in control of this situation and didn't really like it. Jim who knew about Alex approached Catherine and explained

"Well, you have to admit she is good. I mean she is actually perfect for the part and just because she's..."

He never finished, for Catherine had now decided to change her relative embarrassment into a controlling attitude of pronounced command.

"OK, OK, OK," she uttered pushing Jim to one side, "can we get on with this. I'm ready and I know Alex is so let's shoot this scene."

Vicki spoke to a smirking Lester,

"You know she is really good at a situation like this. It's rare that she is ever thrown."

"I know, a wonderful person, quite marvellous," replied Lester admiring his protégé, "I'm really glad I signed her up. She is definitely my very best."

Jim had by now reclaimed his position as director and was standing just off the set, mid centre. He spoke,

"Right... quiet everyone... let's do this in one take... camera... and... action."

Catherine had decided to put everything into this shot. Lesbian or no lesbian, failure and mediocrity were not part of her make-up. Alex had entered the set and had walked up to her.

"You look tired Susan," she muttered slowly removing her dressing gown. The camera went to close-up as they kissed, holding the shot for as long as possible as Catherine's tongue met Alex's. Their mouths were locked together in a long and sensual embrace. Alex started to run her hand up Catherine's back and took a handful of her hair in it. She gently pulled her head back and started to kiss her throat.

Catherine rolled her eyes back and thought, 'For someone who's supposed to be fucking tired she ain't half taking the fucking initiative.'

Alex had brought Catherine onto the bed and had positioned herself kneeling by her head. She smiled at Catherine and then looked directly into the camera. Reaching down over her breasts Alex spread her hand over Catherine's tummy and very slowly and rhythmically pushed down to between her legs. She raised one leg and stroked her thigh, groaning with pleasure as she did so. One camera held on Alex's expressive and lustful face whilst a second moved to capture the masturbation scene. Jim was directing with a calm assurance, Vicki looked on with amazement as her friend accomplished a form of eroticism which was alien to her and Lester started to think about how much of this scene would have to be cut before the film was given a certificate. Alex was over Catherine now, on all fours, gently widening Catherine's legs ensuring that her lover's vagina was exposed completely to the camera.

'This is getting too hard-core,' thought Catherine who knew the difference between eroticism and what was likely to end up as a detailed biological investigation of her private parts. She heaved a reluctant Alex from on top of her and gasped her final lines.

"You're as good as a man any day," whilst thinking to herself, 'God, the things I fucking do for the film industry.' Alex gave her one last parting kiss before the director shouted,

"Cut" to a general round of applause from the camera crew.

Vicki ran up to Catherine laughing loudly and spluttering out her words like a machine gun,

"Cathy you were... hell... What will Victor... hell... bloody heck... that was brilliant... how do you do it..?"

"Shut up Vicki," said an embarrassed Catherine who was moving as fast as possible towards the dressing room door. Lester called out,

"Wonderful lovey, absolutely suuuuuper and all done in one take."

Alex followed Catherine looking happy, whilst Catherine grabbed Vicki for 'protection' as she put it and led her into the dressing room.

"Don't worry darling it's over and thanks very much I enjoyed myself," sighed Alex who was content to wait until Catherine had left the dressing room before she started to put her own clothes on, "that is going to make quite a good shot."

"I thought it was getting too explicit, I mean it left nothing to the imagination," replied Catherine, "they'll probably cut that last bit."

"For the home video store market no doubt but I bet it appears under quite a few counters and on mail order firm's catalogues, it was too good to miss, what with you showing everything you've got and me displaying my all at the same time. Quite good, if I might say so. We have to do another one like that don't we?"

"No we bloody well don't. Your next victim is apparently my sister who married an impotent bloke and they both live next door. Who the hell writes this garbage?"

"I think it's a great idea, you could do a follow-up," joined in Vicki who was hugely enjoying her friend's displeasure, "you could call it 'The Return of the Nympho Lesbian' or 'Lesbian Nymphos Strike Back'."

Catherine was dressing at speed like a mistress who is just about to be caught out by a returning wife.

"More like call it 'Catherine Gives Up Films And Takes Up Nursing'."

She had finished dressing and looked at the still smiling Alex who was sitting on the dressing table with her legs resting on a chair. Catherine thought that she had better say something nice to her because with a bit of editing the scene was going to look quite good,

"I might see you again, and despite you getting too much of a thrill out of me, I thought it went very well."

"Thanks lover, see you next time,"

Alex flicked her hand across her pubic hair and blew a kiss at the retreating Catherine. The pair of friends moved so quickly down the corridor to the exit that when they pushed open the door they sent a relaxed Lester spinning into the gutter.

"Ouch!" said the agent looking up at his assailants, "Oh, it's you two dear hearts. Fancy dumping your agent in the gutter, I don't know."

"Sorry Lester, we didn't see you, are we going for a drink?"

"Yes, but first let's go back to the office and work out what you are going to do after this film. I've turned down two offers for some hard-core stuff but one of the others is a sex comedy and I think you'd like it. It's set in a hospital."

The three characters started to walk towards the cars.

"Sex comedies are either set in hospitals or schools," said Catherine, "but I do prefer them to the porno stuff. It's a bit of a step up for me then Lester?"

"Absolutely cuddle-bundle. It should get you off the top shelf of video shops and onto the main stream."

"Good news. Let's have a drink at your office. We'll follow you in our car."

Within a few minutes they had arrived at Lester's office and were sipping G&T's. Vicki was bubbling with excitement over the filming, asking countless questions and wondering if she could sell Lester a time-share apartment. Catherine was slowly getting drunk whilst Lester was trying to find the script for the sex comedy.

"I'm sure I left it somewhere. Now... where?" he was rummaging around in his filing cabinet, "Ah here it is, now Cathy, take a look..."

His words were never finished. At that moment the jovial and chattering and drunken atmosphere was shattered by an iron crow bar smashing through the glass in Lester's door scattering lethal showers of glass across the floor like an explosion of shrapnel. A second later a man had crashed down the door and had burst into the centre of the room. He was followed rapidly by six other men all armed with crow bars. Hellish violence now erupted onto the tranquil scene.

"Right you bastards don't anybody move or we will crush your fucking heads."

At the sound of the shattering glass Catherine had dived for cover, in the next second Lester had flung himself over her body, by the time they had uttered their threat Vicki was almost through a window and onto the fire escape. An arm pulled her back,

"Not you sweetie," said one of the men, "it's you we want."

She found herself being helplessly thrown against the wall and then felt a blow smashing into her stomach. Without really knowing what was happening her reflexes doubled her over in pain and as she collapsed she received another blow before a powerful kick hammered into her head. Trying to protect herself with her hands she found herself being dragged towards the door. Unable to scream, her last sight had been of one of the men kicking a prostrate Lester whilst another had slammed an iron bar across Catherine's breasts.

Within a minute it was over.

The men lugged a stunned Vicki into a waiting van and sped off towards London Bridge, heading for south of the river. Vicki's first feeling on slowly coming round from her state of shock was one of sickness, her second was one of pain and it was only her third which registered fear. She raised a hand to the back of her head and touched a growing lump; bringing her hand away she could just focus her eyes enough to see that her hand had blood on it. It was this sight rather than the pain which increased her terror and like a prisoner who faced torture from a regime whose only legitimacy came from force she cowered on the floor of the van waiting for the next acts of violence. It was this pause in the physical pain which disturbed her the most giving as it did no respite from the mental torture. Her eyes were now focusing properly and she looked at the four men in the back of the van.

"Hello sweetie," said one, "remember me?"

The voice belonged to one of Nigel's heavies that had been with him in the Grapes,

"We are going to have some fun with you tonight."

Vicki tried to speak, she tried to utter something defiant like the prisoners in those war movies always did, she tried to say 'up yours', but instead she started to cry. The men began to laugh and taunt her but this did not affect her, for once the tears had started to fall she was not aware of anything else except the release they provided. She sobbed as many other victims have cried; not out of self-pity nor out of fear but out of pain and helplessness.

One of the men placed his hand on her thigh and squeezed violently, he was pulled away by the man who had spoken.

"I think Crofty wants a go at it first and then I'm second."

The man then leered at Vicki,

"Yes sweetie, we're going to have a little bit of an orgy tonight and you are going to be the only girl. Just think of it one girl with six blokes. How lucky can you get. But first I think we'll send you to sleep a little. We don't want you to start yelling for help, do we?"

He took a handkerchief from one pocket and a bottle from the other. Applying the liquid generously he placed the handkerchief over her nose and mouth and within five seconds she had blanked out.

At Lester's office Catherine and her agent moved towards each other in shock at the quickness, precision and sadism of the violence. Both had experienced violence of a kind before, but it was pub violence or it was an argument followed by a fight on a film set. Yet neither had ever undergone this calculating mobster violence which had no rules of fighting, aiming blows at whatever part of the body was closest and which left the victims bereft of any sense of what to do next. Even in the most violent of pub fights there was a certain morality of when to leave a victim alone and there was always somebody to stop the fight. Yet here there was nobody to turn to, nobody to pull the fighting factions apart. This was the kind of violence in which there was no end until one side was destroyed.

Lester spoke first, words which he thought sounded completely banal,

"Are you OK?" His voice had dropped the hyperbolic accent of earlier.

"I suppose so. They've taken Vicki."

"Do we phone the police?"

"No!" said Catherine who was aware enough of what was going on to realise that police involvement was their last resort.

"No, we phone Victor and get him and the rest of them up here."

Lester handed Catherine the 'phone whilst he looked at the broken door. He heard Catherine explain in broken sentences what had happened and waited for her to put the 'phone down.

"Victor says don't phone the police he's going to get everyone up here."

She stood up and carefully moved around the slivers of broken glass. Placing a comforting hand on Lester's shoulder she said,

"I'm sorry you got involved in this. You see I recognised two of the blokes who did it, I know who they are."

"So do I, and don't apologise, because you see it's partly my fault. I'll tell you when everyone gets here. Do you want to clean yourself up whilst I try and get this place back into shape?"

At moments of crises Lester always believed that he could come out with a joke or a quip or a one liner which would make everyone laugh and make everyone feel better but on this occasion he suddenly didn't feel like joking or laughing; the assault on his office had left him shaken and feeling vulnerable. He had once had his home burgled and that had left him feeling distraught at the thought that criminals had gone through his things, breaking and throwing them around his flat. But this was more evil, being completely planned and being carried out with a cold ruthlessness. Catherine came back and they sat waiting for the rest of the Class to arrive drinking large quantities of brandy to alleviate the pain.

Victor, the Lawyer, Pete, Louise and Dave arrived quickly, breaking speed limits and jumping traffic lights. Catherine could only sigh deeply on seeing Victor and point towards Vicki's jacket which was still hanging on the door. The details of the assault were quickly explained and Lester added the following,

"I knew about this group from their activities in King's Cross, word soon gets around. I didn't want you to get involved with them because of their reputation and because the police are starting to get wind of a major child pornography, banned video and drugs business. I had an inspector round here not too long ago, about last month asking questions about any film company that might be making illicit videos. At the time I didn't associate the group which had broken the Notario family in King's Cross with a child sex racket but then things started to develop. You see one of them came to me and asked if I had any girls on my books who would do things out of the ordinary. That, by the way, usually means with animals or other nasty things. I said 'no' and then he asked if I handled younger girls. You see he'd seen a young girl come in here, you know Catherine, the one I mentioned. When I said I didn't he obviously thought that I was stalling, waiting for an offer of a large commission. So he offered it to me, a thumping great amount if I could get hold of any girls between the ages of 12 and 15. He also wanted me to line up a film crew who would be prepared to take high quality films. I said 'no' again and he suddenly left. About two hours later I was visited by the bloke Vicki knows with two of his heavies who warned me not to talk about it to anyone. So I didn't. I think what happened was that when you lot lifted the videos from their transit store they thought that I might have lagged to the police, giving a description etc., so they watched my office."

"And saw Vicki and me enter with you," groaned Catherine.

"Why did they pick on your agency in the first place?" asked Victor. "You seem to be pretty legit to me."

"With films I am and with Catherine I am. But you see I can also get girls for clubs in the West End and some of my girls go abroad to Denmark and places. So you see, while I'm on the level I also have wide interests and get known in various places."

"So what you are saying," said Louise in a slightly angry tone, "is that you also run a call-girl business."

"No, no, no, I haven't explained myself clearly. The girls I send abroad and the girls who dance in the West End might get up to other things. I don't ask questions, you know that, Catherine. I didn't know what you got up to outside of the dancing."

"I can put you right there," interrupted Catherine, "I was sleeping, completely knackered out, and I was sleeping with Victor."

"Look I don't want to get into a discussion on the morality of what dancers get up to or don't get up to, it's not Lester's responsibility and it's not ours," said Victor. "We have got to work out how to find Vicki and how to smash these bastards."

At that moment the 'phone rang and Lester picked up the receiver.

"...you got Vicki..." he was interrupted by Victor snatching the phone from him.

"Either you bloody well give her back or I'll bloody well cut your bloody throats you wankers."

The clipped accents of Croft-White came across the line.

"Now calm down Manning. I have a straight business proposition to make to you. We want the films and you want Vicki. A straight swap. No strings, no problems and no police. What do you say?"

"We could go straight to the cops right now, kidnapping and child pornography charges should send you lot down for a very long time."

"If we go we take you and your group with us. We also arrange for an accident for Vicki. As you say the charges are so serious that we might as well take a risk that they will never find the body. Oh yes, and our spies tell me that you have been talking to a couple of very silly men from Southwark, well they will go as well if you don't comply."

Victor felt momentarily trapped.

"OK a swap. Tell me the time and place."

Details were exchanged and the phone put down. Victor turned to the group,

"How the bloody hell did they know about Arthur and his son?"

"Well, it was John who came charging out of the pub and told me to run," explained Charlie, "Sorry."

"Not your fault, can't be helped. Right then, we will have to plan."

Catherine joined in the discussion,

"The first thing is we have to ensure Vicki's safety above all else and I think we'd better tell Arthur and John what we're up to."

"You're correct of course," said Victor, "but I've just worked out what to do. They have left a door through which we walk."

Chapter 19

Inspector Benjamin was getting nowhere with his interrogation of the mobsters. They were past masters of deceit and falsehoods which left him wondering if bringing back torture would not be a good way of extracting a confession.

"We'll hold them for as long as possible before charging them with any disorder offence we can find," he said to Campbell, "but at least a pattern is starting to emerge. We know that their mob is somehow involved in a punch-up with Victor's alchy group and we know that they're operating from the Grapes. They'll probably expect us to start monitoring the pub so let's not disappoint them. We also know that Charlie had a rather bad slash across his face which will need hospital treatment, so get on to the local hospitals and see if anything has come up. Shouldn't be too hard to spot, a knife wound on a Monday lunch time has to be pretty rare."

Campbell left the room and a fellow officer came in waving a report:

"They might not talk but their prints do. Two of them have records a mile long."

Benjamin quickly scanned the report.

"Usual stuff, violence, menace, petty theft, public order offence and latest known activities... part of a gang run by... well, well, well... find out all you can about this character. I think he fronts a nightclub in Camden. We'll start to lean on him today."

There were three times when he found police work thoroughly rewarding: when he had just found out some information which would lead to a bust; when the bust had been successfully completed, and when the criminals were put behind bars. Well, actually there was a fourth and that was at the Christmas party when the W.P.C.s let their hair down, but that was another matter. Now he was feeling the first signs of success. The lead to the public school drop-out would soon force the gang either to lie low which would give him time to gather evidence and proceed with some sort of case or it would force them into the open, to take risks and to expose their operation. He thought that the latter might be the case. Campbell came back with the news that he had hoped for.

"Yep, he's at the hospital. I've got the car waiting, are we going now?"

"Of course. I think our man Charlie might be ready to talk."

Charlie was meanwhile being wheeled down a long corridor towards one of the surgery rooms. He felt a bit foolish being pushed along by John and holding a mop of cotton wool to his face. He could have walked just as easily but the nurse had muttered something about going into a state of shock and to be honest he was beginning to feel a bit sick. The wound had been deep but had also been clean, the knife had been razor sharp and the junior doctor was suitably impressed with the precision of the cut.

"I cut myself shaving," remarked Charlie.

"Wonderful what these modern razors will do," said the doctor, "I could have sworn that this was a knife wound."

"Yes, well, it was actually. I was cutting some balsawood for my son's model aircraft and the knife slipped."

It didn't sound convincing and it wasn't meant to. It was more of a 'could we get on with it' type of explanation which he hoped would silence any more questions.

"Well then, I'm going to inject a little local anaesthetic which will make your face go numb, rather like at the dentist and could you..."

"Not look because I might be sick. I used to be a hospital porter so I know the drill. The last time somebody stuck a needle into me I threw up and then fainted so my eyes are going firmly tight."

The injection completed without Charlie being sick or fainting the doctor cleaned the wound and then waited a few seconds before putting in the stitches. It was finished quite quickly and with no pain. At the end the doctor said

"Rest here for about half and hour would you. A nurse will come in and just make sure that everything is alright."

"You're going to have one hell of a scar," said John who had been waiting outside.

"Yes my friend, quite a war wound!"

It was Benjamin who spoke following John into the room. Charlie groaned in a half-hearted fashion as the police officer sat down.

"I thought it was you in the car, thanks for arriving on time and for slamming the door into that bloke. It stopped him dead."

"Your thanks are appreciated as would be some answers to my questions."

He wasn't sure if it was the effects of the anaesthetic or whether he was feeling genuinely pleased to see Benjamin but Charlie was about to be cooperative. It was John who interrupted,

"Look, you can't expect Charlie to make sense after the shock and the drug and all that. The stuff he's had injected into you makes you go a bit ga-ga. When I had it I started swearing my head off, right in the middle of the ward. The doctor had to have me shifted to another ward, less public. As for information it would be next to useless. Why not wait? I'll phone Victor and see if we can't get a meeting or something. Would that do OK?"

Benjamin could feel that the balance of events were turning decisively his way. It was that rare moment in the solving of a crime when the balance of forces was beginning to shift, was beginning to create a momentum that would ultimately gather pace and race towards a successful conclusion. There were many aspects of life that were like this: a cricket match when the taking of a wicket would start a collapse; a general election when a false comment or a bad day would start a party on the road to defeat; or even a seduction when at the right moment a reluctant girlfriend might be turned into an expectant lover. Benjamin had concluded that life was a series of coincidences and events which made up a momentum either for success or failure. Those who were successful in life realised this and seized the moments of promise. This was one such moment. The fact that Victor might just now talk was to be encouraged. He patted Charlie on the back.

"Well, warrior, you get your boss to meet me at the station and we'll see what happens."

Charlie was grinning in reply, the effects of the anaesthetics were really making him quite jolly, but it was John who replied.

"How about a more neutral setting? Like a pub?"

"Like the Lamb and Flag," added Charlie.

"Like the alchies' hide away, responded Benjamin. "OK the pub it is!"

That evening the pub was almost deserted. The landlord had

opened earlier to start a barbecue in the pub's garden. A few regulars had arrived and were milling around outside, clutching their pints and generally getting in the way of the preparations. In one corner of the garden a country and western singer was rehearsing her songs. The stage from the pub had been moved outside and a couple of the singer's friends were putting up the microphone and testing the sound. It was not an evening for sitting in doors, but Victor was there, in his corner with his fruit juice waiting for Benjamin. Catherine and the Lawyer were with him sipping G&Ts, Catherine thinking of the possibility of an open air strip. All three were strangely elated at the thought of the forthcoming meeting: Victor because it meant he could joust against a policeman; the Lawyer because it meant a deal might be struck and he liked dealing and deals; and Catherine because the meeting might just start in process a series of moves which could get Vicki back.

Victor had developed something of a plan. It would at best lead to the posh bastards being smashed, Vicki's return, the Class getting away with past crimes and John getting an amnesty from a possible drugs charge, or it could at worse lead to the Class and John being done by the police and Vicki being done by the posh bastards. It would, however, ultimately lead to Croft-White's operation being smashed.

They did not have long to wait. Benjamin and Campbell arrived at five past seven, bought a round of drinks and sat down. Benjamin spoke first,

"Right Manning, this is how I see it. You and your lot are engaged in some quite ropy business, some definite crimes in fact. You have also been implicated with a gang operating out of London that are involved in a possible child sex ring and pornography and possibly drugs. Let me warn you that any withholding of evidence is a crime and we'll sling everything at you."

Although he spoke in low terms and attempted to add a chilling tone to his voice Victor sat poker-faced against this threat. John's idea of holding the meeting in a pub had been a masterstroke, the atmosphere dampened any real menace. However, Victor was playing events calmly, he wanted the highest option for the Class and John.

"Look Benjamin," he said, "I know you have to threaten us like that and tell us our rights should you want to bloody well arrest us, but you see, you could have bloody well done that a couple of days ago. So let's just have a chat and try and work something out. We have a major problem."

"Go on."

"Well, this gang of morons are attempting to push us out of our video and electronic business which is bloody well not on."

Catherine wished Victor could have a drink, the 'bloodies' were creating the wrong impression.

"You see, we bloody well built this business up from nothing and it's going to be a bloody good pension for me in the future."

"And how are they attempting to push you out. Violence?"

"Not really."

At this stage Victor was not going to admit anything which could lead to a shift away from his original ideas.

"They are flooding the market with cut price videos. You know, just like when the buses were bloody privatised, with fares being slashed so that one company after another was forced out, leaving one major one which could hike their fares up again."

"And you expect me to believe that a bunch like you lot are going to let a group of drop-outs take you over without a fight. Come off it. I'll tell you what I think. I think you've been leant on and pretty badly. You were beaten up along with Dave Watson and now Charlie has been carved. I also think that we are talking about the same group here and let me make it quite clear that I want those bunch of child porno merchants busted."

As a duel of words the conversation was quite unusual. Both combatants were restrained, both were holding back and yet both knew that they would cooperate in the end. Victor held the advantage; he knew the time of the swap and he knew that Benjamin had no knowledge of Vicki. He desperately did not want the police to know about the kidnapping just yet because he did not trust them, he had heard of too many instances of the police fouling-up kidnapping cases and he also wanted revenge. A revenge which would be outside the law had to be kept from the law. The law would ultimately protect the posh bastards from any real punishment, the kind of physical torture which they had inflicted on the Class, and Victor wanted that, he wanted revenge. And so he started to spin a tale for the policeman.

"All right then I'll bloody well tell you what is going on and then I want to make a deal."

"No promises, but I'll see what you say."

"Right, last week we were done in by that lot, they are using muscle to force us out. So last night we done their warehouse in Southwark and lifted their videos."

This was the first gamble and the first admission of a crime. Benjamin appeared not to be interested in the break in, he leant across to Campbell and whispered some words to him before replying,

"What sort of videos?"

"Legit and some kiddie porn. So yes, you're right, that lot are perverts."

"And I suppose you want immunity from prosecution for breaking and entering?"

"That for starters."

"Have you anything to link the videos with the drop-outs?"

"No. but we will have. You see they have evidence on us and on John Wilson from Southwark, you know the bloke who is a mate of Charlie's."

That was a partial lie, but on no account was Victor going to reveal Vicki's kidnapping. The pace of the conversation accelerated as both men knew that they were reaching agreement. A bond began to develop between them, of two unlikely figures from differing backgrounds coming together for common gain. With his military analogies Victor thought it was like Hitler and Stalin coming together to sign the Nazi-Soviet pact; Hitler so that he could turn against the West and Stalin so that he could preserve the Soviet Union and develop his strength for a final conflict. He continued,

"They know about a couple of little things that we did in the past, a couple of minor little incidents that were slightly outside the law."

"What, you mean the time-share business and the importing of antiques from the USA without a licence?"

The fact that the police knew about this came as a surprise. The Lawyer was half on his feet, and not being very good at hiding his emotions burst out,

"How the hell did you know about that? We would have got the licence, it was only a matter of time. It was important to get them in fast in time for the auction."

That was the truth but it was always difficult using the truth to justify a crime.

"We know about it because we are paid to know about it and we were going to see you but you, with all due respects, are small fry. Customs officials are more worried about stolen art treasures being lifted from Italy than with a small-time business in Kent. And before you mention Charlie, will you show me a second-hand car salesman who operates one hundred per cent within the law. They are very rare."

Victor was slightly shocked by this admission of the policeman's. He suddenly realised that he had perhaps been living in an idealised world where the police cracked down on every crime or, where they didn't, they were on the payroll of a local firm. To hear a police officer effectively admit that there were now grades of crimes and that some were not really worth investigating opened up new possibilities for him. He suddenly saw room for expansion, extending the twilight world of his activities just a little bit further into the dodgy. He was like a man who for most of his life has never been in debt, who has deprived himself of many pleasures just to try and build up a reputation with the bank for being a good customer. Then he meets the bank manager who effectively tells him that debt is fine and acceptable and even if he went over his borrowing limit all that would occur would be a slap on the wrist and an expectation that he would be putting some money back in. The man then stops worrying about money and starts to enjoy himself, slowly building up a debt, gradually increasing his limit until the unwritten rules say 'no more'. Well, Victor became aware of the fact that he hadn't reached his limit, that a little more bending of the rules would be permissible. Inside he felt pleased by this lifting of one threat and at least it seemed as if Dave and Louise's computer frauds had not been discovered, but his face did not show this pleasure, it remained expressionless, even though he felt that he held all four aces.

"There is one more thing that they have against us. It's about John Wilson. They are quite capable of framing him for drug pushing. He has a bloody record already for possession."

Once again for Benjamin this was no problem and he told Victor that John would be cleared if he was innocent. Benjamin wanted the proof of the connection between the videos and the firm.

"Right, this is bloody well it. They want to do a swap. They want their videos for the information they have on us."

Benjamin was delighted with this news, Campbell got another round of drinks.

"What is time and place of the swap?"

Victor gave the time and place of the swap but he gave the wrong time (it was due to take place ten minutes earlier), and he gave the wrong venue (it was fixed for a location about a mile away).

"Now, as we've been very cooperative with you could you tell us what will be the position about the past, shall we call them 'bloody mistakes'?"

"The position is that we are not interested in those minor cases. The police force is overstretched as it is without running around chasing you lot. Just give Campbell here, as your local friendly bobby a promise that you will all be good boys and girls in the future."

"Agreed," said the Lawyer.

"Agreed," said Victor.

They were both lying and they knew that Campbell appreciated this but at the moment it did not matter.

"This is therefore what will happen. You will hand over the videos nice and peacefully,"

'Nice and peaceful my foot,' mused Victor to himself as Benjamin continued,

"and we will wait until they are in full possession and then we'll nab them."

"What about the information on the child sex ring and the production of these videos?" Catherine asked.

"Apart from being perverted they are also giving us legit erotic movie actresses a bad name."

"Don't worry about that. With the information you've given us we'll be able to get a warrant. We'll hit their night club and their offices at the same time as the swap is taking place. We'll have enough to send this lot down for some time. The drugs' bust will be easy."

The police officers rose to leave. The pub was still empty but outside the barbecue was proceeding happily and the singer had just started her first song. The words of 'Country Roads' interrupted their talk.

"I quite like pub singing," said Benjamin, "and, by the way, when this is over how about you coming to London to a policeman's stag night, we need a good dancer."

Catherine agreed and placed the date in her diary as Benjamin and

Campbell left the pub. They almost collided with Pete who bounded through the door with a happy smile playing on his lips and who looked as if he wanted to say something. Catherine's motions told him to shut up until the police had left. After they had gone Pete told them that the vehicles were ready for the swap and that Charlie, John, Dave and Louise were waiting outside.

"Get them in," said Victor. "I've got something to explain."

A loud shout of laughter came from the garden breaking into the singer's music. The barbecue was a big success. Victor looked at the Lawyer,

"Look I know what you're thinking. Why the bloody hell didn't I tell them about Vicki and why the bloody hell did I give them the wrong time and place?"

The Lawyer nodded and Catherine added,

"Yes, that's about the size of it. We were in the clear. You heard him, they aren't interested in us."

The rest of the Class entered and after getting their drinks they sat down. The Lawyer explained what had happened and John said,

"You're taking a big risk here Victor, but in the time I've known you there must be a reason."

"There is. Look, I don't trust them to deal with Vicki's kidnapping. I mean I know they've been bloody good at tracing some of the kids who have gone missing and been kidnapped over the last few years but there have been other bloody occasions when they bloody well haven't and the girl has been found dead. I want us to handle this. We are going to hit those bastards with everything we've got. Pete's been going round the pubs this lunchtime getting our regulars ready and we think we have enough to really hit them. What we do is we get a firm together and arrive before time. We get Vicki out of their clutches and then we smash into them. I want a real ruck, I want everyone to come tooled up, this is going to be bloody heavy. Then with about five minutes to spare Catherine phones the police to tell them of the change of venue and they arrive to find the posh bastards badly bloody beaten and in possession of kiddie porn."

It was a brilliant plan as everyone agreed. Revenge would be part of this operation. The Lawyer, although not a fighter himself could immediately see the effects of this strategy.

"It means nobody will dare bother with us again."

"Right," said Victor. "I know that we have always avoided

violence because violence does not always pay but there are times when the Class is going to have to fight and this is bloody one of them."

Pete was getting excited.

"I've got my baseball bat," he said gesticulating a swing with it that would knock any ball out of the ball park.

"Good for you. Now, we get everyone together and start to move up towards Southwark. Here's where we meet."

He gave them all a piece of paper.

"We move in separate groups. John you go back home and see if you can't get some heavies together, but keep it quiet. Pete, you get the mob out of the Eagle and Child, and get Jagdish and his Asian heavies out of The Bookbinders. Dave, you go to the King's Arms and the White Horse. Louise, phone up Chris at the Union bar he's waiting to give the message to some heavies who owe me a favour. I'm going to call every favour in that I'm owed. You Lawyer and Charlie go to the Ruskin Arms and try and drag out every one of those boozy bastards; if we can get that lot moving we've won."

The commands were given and the Class rose determined to pull out every measure they could. They left Catherine and Victor alone.

"We're going to hit those bloody wankers and hit them hard. Like bloody panzer tanks we'll be."

"And what then are we going to do?" she said.

"We are going up to Dartford to see some old friends of mine at the Black Boy Pub. Friends from a long time ago who still owe me a few favours, friends who are still willing to lend me a hand. They are the hardest bunch of bastards you will ever see and they smash anyone for a price."

Chapter 20

While Victor was explaining the plan to the rest of the Class Vicki was slowly becoming aware of pain and something cutting into her wrists. She was lying on her side on the rough and grimy wooden floor of what looked like a store house. Her eyes were level with the floor and she stared at the grains on the wood not fully comprehending where she was or what had happened. She groaned and rolled over onto her back and stared at the ceiling gradually becoming conscious of her surroundings. She sat up and looked around her. The vault of a room was empty except for a table at one end, there were no windows and the only entrance was a large double door at the side. An unshaded lightbulb hung from the centre and brightly lit up the four corners of the room. In one corner were dumped her own clothes and she looked down at what she was wearing; it was the school girl's uniform which Nigel had wanted her to wear. The clothes didn't fit, being too small but the implications of these clothes for Vicki became clear as she fearfully imagined the violence that was to come. She became aware that her hands were tied too tightly behind her. The rope was cutting into her flesh and she was also aware of the aches from the beating she had received. Her mouth was dry and she felt as if she could drink a river. At that moment the doors were pushed open and standing in the evening sunlight were a group of men, some of whom she knew and one she knew very well. It was the latter's voice which spoke.

"Don't think I'm going to gloat sweetie and come out with such corny lines as 'so we meet again' because wanker I am going to hurt you badly."

It was the clipped accents of Croft-White who came towards her with a menacing stare. As he walked by her he kicked her in the side and she rolled away from him into a corner. The other men came in and the doors were closed. The atmosphere was expectant with evil and like a prisoner awaiting their execution Vicki felt that every second before the dawn was precious. Her thoughts were now perfectly concentrated, her mind had sharpened, trying to work out how she was going to get out of this situation. She huddled in the corner and drew her knees up to her chest. Nigel sat on the table whilst the men stood in a semi circle around her and she noticed that one of them was carrying a cane.

"Two things are going to happen," said Nigel. "First of all we want our tapes back. So what we are going to do is to trade you for the tapes. However, before that we are going to have a little bit of fun. I paid for you to act the school girl and now I'm claiming my goods. So we are going to have a little game of role play."

Two of the men grabbed her under each arm and dragged her unwilling body towards the table.

"That's right, don't come wanting it. You see a bit of struggle helps the atmosphere. After all you have been a naughty girl and now you are going to be punished."

At last for Vicki she found the defiance which had earlier eluded her.

"You fucking queers. Get off on little girls do you, it'll be little boys and sheep next."

She was pushed face down on the table, her chest painfully crushed beneath her. One of the men was leaning down hard on her shoulders and had wedged her face between his legs. She felt suffocated and sick but a resilience had entered her, telling her that she was going to survive. Memories of her childhood rocketed into her mind, of her uncle, of that Saturday night and of the loss of innocence. Her skirt was being lifted, her knickers were being roughly pulled down, and her buttocks were being painfully squeezed. Setting herself against the torture she tried to shut out the pain of the slaps against her, she didn't cry out.

"Little girlie not crying, little girlie needs to be caned."

Croft-White swung the cane and hit her, cutting into her flesh and drawing blood.

"Not too much blood, don't want blood on our willies do we boys?"

The rape lasted for five minutes. Minutes in which social morality and human decency fell against an onslaught of sadistic violence and barbarous perversion. After each act of rape they hit her and punched her; the torment crashed over Vicki, tearing her body with searing pain. Inside she felt like an inferno, the burning heat rending her, quartering her, slashing at her with a ferocity that was Mephistophelean in its intensity. She craved peace and was immobilised not only by the physical restraints but by a longing for release.

It came, finally, and was accompanied by several blows to her face and groin before they threw her from the table and into a corner like a dead sacrificial victim.

"Delightful, absolutely delightful," leered Nigel. "now I'm going to telephone your friends and arrange for a deal. And I do hope that they won't go to the police because if they do you are dead and they will go to prison for naughty crimes."

"And you'll fucking rot in hell," hissed Vicki who had once again found her voice. "You can shag sheep as much as you like there."

She was at her most sarcastic,

"It's almost as perverted as your minds."

Seb Austen closed in on her, eyes throwing out hatred, Vicki managed to raise a knee to protect herself before a kick caught her in the chest.

"That's enough Seb. You know Vicki, when this little incident is over we might continue the war. I don't like lippy sluts like you and I am beginning to get real pleasure out of inflicting pain. I can see what the Marquis De Sade saw in it. The slow torture and the absolute pleasure."

"The Marquis De Fucking who?" answered Vicki, "one of your foreign perverts was he?"

"Ignore her Nigel, let's make the phone call and arrange the swap."

They left her in the dark and a new pain hit her; the terror of isolation and the fear of future torture. She also badly wanted to go to the toilet but any compassion from this lot was unthinkable.

'Now I know what hostage victims go through' she thought as she relieved herself lying on the floor, the urine soaked through her knickers and made a pool on the floor.

Strangely enough it was this act which helped her to come to terms with her situation. There were no rules of decency in times of real violence. There was no 'Geneva Convention' for captives. There was only the whims and fancies of a group of people who had left the charade of human decency far behind them. There was no civilisation here and no laws, all had been deserted in the movement towards the savage. This thought freed her to some extent. She began to realise that apart from the pain, which was subsiding, the most terrifying aspect was the thought that 'good' had been discarded and 'evil' had taken its place. 'Evil' had become the norm. The rape and the torture had been an attempt to assert mastery and to break her. But what if she treated it as being the norm? What if she accepted that violence would be part of the situation? It was as if she was involved in a fight with another person. In fights there are always clearly defined rules. There are always the conventions which prevent you from going for lethal blows and there are social rules which say that you mustn't kick a person when they're down. There were laws which said that there was justified self-defence but also laws which could turn self-defence into manslaughter, just like that man who had carried a sword-stick on a train to protect himself against muggers and when he was attacked successfully defended himself against the attackers. He had been charged with possession of an offensive weapon. But what if those rules had been changed? What if the situation now had become one in which there were no social conventions? She could accept the violence and then plan retaliation. The pain would go, the psychological scar could be fought against and anyway it was not as bad as the hurt she had received as a child. The thoughts came quickly, flooding into her, attempting to create a justification.

Vicki rationalised along these lines and she began to feel better. She now knew that this gang was desperate and that they might kill her because child pornography plus kidnapping would send them down for a long time. The fear of death was with her but not the fear of torture or rape. She would get her revenge.

Events were starting to move quickly. Benjamin and Campbell had made the arrangements for the bust and were beginning to move into position, the Class and their heavies were speeding towards Southwark and Victor and Catherine had arrived at the Black Boy.

"What a fucking dive!" said Catherine as they entered the pub.

"This is bloody brilliant, one of the few bars of its kind left."

Victor pushed open the door of the public bar and ushered Catherine in. The bar was a very old fashioned spit and sawdust affair. The walls were tiled,

"To make it easy to wash the blood off from a Saturday night punch up," explained Victor.

There were no seats and only long wooden benches with the male drinkers slumped over their pints on long wooden tables. A broken bar billiards table stood in one corner and the barman leaned on the bar taking snuff. This was the kind of pub where a stranger either left quickly or drank his pint avoiding all eye contact.

'This is worse than the Rochester pubs,' thought Catherine. 'This is introverted, this is hostile.'

The bar had gone quiet as they walked in but then the atmosphere changed as one powerfully built man recognised Victor.

"How's tricks, Victor?" He asked slowly and with a drunken drawl.

"Not bad Andy, I want to talk some business. I need some heavies."

"Fine. Count us in for a price. But before we talk, get the woman out of here."

Victor looked at Catherine who was about to utter something about sexism when she thought the better of it and said instead,

"Right, I'll just get a packet of crisps and sit outside in the car."

The irony of treating her like an underage person being asked to leave was lost on the company who seemed content to see her go. She had only a few minutes to wait before Victor followed by eight other men spilled out of the pub and into the car park. Victor climbed in and Catherine started the engine.

"I thought you took that very well," said Victor. "I thought you were going to have a go at them."

"Listen lover, I can handle pretty well every type of bloke but that lot are a throw back to another era. I mean they're bloody Neanderthal."

"I know, the sort of bloke who won wars for this country and made it great. Anyway, we've got them coming. Bloody hell they're a dangerous mob. It'll cost us fifty each."

"Four hundred pounds. That's quite good."

"It's like I said they owe me from a previous favour. Right go fairly slowly because they'll be following."

By midnight they were in place. The Class had managed to turn out in force and in total there were about thirty heavies, all well armed; they waited in their cars before moving to the meeting place.

At 1.45am Nigel kicked Vicki who had managed to start dozing and had woken her.

"God, you slut, you stink of piss."

Vicki lashed out with her feet but only succeeded in kicking the wall. They dragged her up and pushed her towards the door.

"What's this, more perverted stuff?" jeered Vicki. Her body was still feeling pain but she was starting to fight back.

"No slut we are going to exchange you for our tapes. If you dare make one false move Seb here will blow your brains out."

Austen had indeed pointed a gun at her head. The threat seemed somewhat far away, almost as if this was a film. Vicki was no longer afraid and was looking first of all for a way of escape and then for a way to hit back. She was marched towards the van and hauled inside. There were nine other men in the back and Vicki was forced to lie on the floor. Another van was behind them full of Croft-White's men. Austen got in behind her, settled himself on a seat and placed his feet on her bum.

"Turn you on, do I?" he said applying pressure to her buttocks.

"No you don't, and may I say by the way that when you stuck your prick inside of me it was about three inches too small."

The other men burst into laughter, Austen's eyes glared with hatred.

"Why you little..."

"Come on Seb," Croft-White's voice came from the front of the van, "she's only trying to wind you up."

The movement of the van brought the talking to a standstill as they moved towards the meeting place. Seb Austen all the time sat quietly staring at nothing and brooding. He was beginning to really hate Vicki.

"OK everyone here's the plan." Nigel Croft-White started to explain what they were going to do. "There won't be any police there but nevertheless be careful. We get out of the van and I want people to line up ready, in case of trouble. Our vans will be parked in the square and I want you Seb and you Dominic to move towards them as soon as we get out. Use your gun if you have to Seb to threaten them but don't shoot unless you have to. If they quietly leave the vans then they get slut back. If not we grab her and head away fast. Hammer and Marco will look after the vans. I've phoned my old mate Brownslow and he's bringing up a few friends. Should be quite fun. Any questions?"

"Why don't we just fucking do them over?" pleaded Austen.

"Quite simply because I want those vans cleared and I don't want any of our people injured. Remember the four blokes in that firm are quite capable of doing harm. Get it? We get in and get out fast. We might hit them another day."

At 1.55am they were in the square. Hammer looked around him and commented,

"Didn't you say your mates would be here, the travellers. Don't look like it, does it."

Croft-White looked unconcerned.

"We really don't need them. How many of us? 16? More than enough, I just thought it might be useful in case a couple of Manning's drunk pub bores turn up with him."

At the travellers' camp Brownslow and the gaunt youth rolled a joint.

"It really wasn't on," said Brownslow.

The two vans containing the videos were parked in plain view. The Class were milling around three cars, their heavies were about a hundred yards away in a side street. As they saw the opposition approach the Lawyer used his personal phone to tell Benjamin that at the last minute the venue had been changed and the swap was taking place now. He then went back into one of the cars and sat there, having phoned their own vans and leaving the lines open. Victor's mind was concentrating on the approaching vans, he knew that they had only five minutes to deal with this lot before the police arrived. He was like an ancient commander of bowmen who would calmly wait until the enemy was upon them before giving the order to fire.

The two vans stopped and Croft-White got out. Seb followed him and then out came Dominic and the men with Vicki being dragged to the front. Victor muttered something under his breath. Nobody heard him. Catherine spoke more audibly.

"Fuck me, look at Vicki. She looks awful."

Austen and Davidson moved towards the vans, Croft-White untied Vicki and pulled her, holding tightly, towards Victor. He spoke,

"Right Manning, here's your slut, we'll just check the films are OK."

Austen and Davidson looked in the back of the vans and called out that everything appeared to be there. Seb climbed into one van and Dominic the other; they started the engines.

"Right you can have her," Croft-White pushed Vicki towards the group.

The Lawyer spoke down the phone:

"Now, now, now, hit them hard."

The screaming sound of engines and screeching wheels crashed down the road, cutting through the still of the night and immediately creating hope for Victor and confusion for Croft- White. On getting her freedom Vicki spun round and charged at the startled Croft-White, slamming a kick into his groin. He half doubled up more in shock than in pain. He backed off and shouted,

"Get those fucking vans out of here."

Seb Austen who had started to get out of the van at the first sign of trouble hesitated and glanced at Davidson who was starting the motor of the second van. He fired a shot at random, hitting nobody. The headlights of the Class' cars shone out through the night like the eyes of enraged beasts charging their enemies. Victor's voice rang out,

"Take the bloody posh bastards."

He didn't have to give this word of command for Charlie and Dave had flung themselves at Croft-White and had brought him down whilst Pete thundered towards the line of men waving his baseball bat and screaming wildly. With the first blow he smashed Hammer across his head, splitting it wide open and sending the man spinning against the side of the van. Davidson's van sped towards them but at that moment the first of the heavies' cars swerved into view, catching Davidson's van on the fender and forcing it to smash into their own van. Austen had stopped trying to start the second van and was scrambling for his gun, a kick to his throat from Victor left him gasping for breath, sprawled out on the floor. The rest of the heavies arrived and poured out of their cars, punching, kicking, swinging iron piping, stabbing with knives and slashing with razor blades. Charlie and Vicki taking it in turns at kicking the by now almost unconscious Croft-White. Dave had hurled Marco across the bonnet of one of the vans, had jumped over it himself and landed both feet on the prostrate Marco's head. Victor was smashing Austen against the side of the van, kicking him more and more rapidly as Austen sank to the ground and Pete, having run out of human enemies had started to smash the windows of Croft-White's van. His own men were scattering along the road, desperate for escape. The regulars from the Black Boy had calmly blocked the other end of the road and waited for them. What happened next was out of Victor's vision, but he heard it; the terrified shouts of Croft-White's men coming up against the determined and directed violence of the boozers from the Black Boy. Croft-White's men were slashed, kicked and smashed with an unrelenting fury. Within two minutes it was over. Catherine watched the massacre taking place at the other end of the road.

"Fucking brilliant!" she breathed.

Victor, gasping for breath aimed one last punch at Austen who crumpled on the ground. Standing for one moment and breathing hard Victor screamed out,

"Let's get the bloody hell out of here. Bloody fast. Move."

They threw themselves back into their cars which lurched into action, the first car managed to crash into a telephone box before careering off down the road whilst Pete's car hurtled across a front drive way as it tried to regain its course. The other cars disappeared into the night. Behind them they could just hear the sound of police sirens entering the square.

"A bloody good night's work that," said Victor. Catherine was looking after Vicki.

"I think we had better get her to the hospital for a thorough check-up."

Vicki gave a halting and stammered reply,

"I'd also like to get out of these fucking clothes," and as if to minimise the pain she was beginning to feel again she added "I hope you realise that I had to wet myself. Those bastards wouldn't let me use the loo."

"Never mind, you can ask Pete out now can't you."

"Talking of whom," said Victor. "Did you see him move. Now

that is what I call a cavalry charge. It scattered them alright."

"More like an elephant charge!" replied Catherine.

"Don't knock elephants," answered Vicki, "they have suddenly become my favourite animals."

She managed a smile, although the effort hurt her cut lip. The breaking of the tense atmosphere brought relief inside the vehicle.

Epilogue

The next Saturday Victor sat in his corner in the near deserted Lamb and Flag. As with all Saturday lunch times that would change by about 1.00pm, just before the stripper arrived in fact. He was enjoying a gentle lunch time session with the rest of the Class, the Lawyer had just sold several valuable pieces of furniture and was standing several rounds. Pete was wearing some new clothes bought for him by his new girlfriend, Vicki, who had told him that she was going to look after him now. He sat very contentedly rocking slowly backwards and forwards in his chair. Charlie was chatting to the landlord who was doing his best to appear cheerful in front of his regulars, although he had heard rumours of a violent confrontation involving them and some gang from up London. He had, on Victor's assurance, just put them down to rumours, but even so he wondered. Louise and Dave were playing some silly drinking game, the rules of which they were beginning to forget as they became more and more drunk. The regulars were starting to arrive in ones and twos quite quickly filling the bar with smoke and laughter. Then through the door walked Benjamin and Campbell.

'Trouble,' thought Victor.

"We've had it now," said the Lawyer.

Benjamin approached their table.

"Can we have a few words gents."

"Of course, sit down. Don't want to alarm the rest of the pub." replied Victor whose face immediately assumed its poker expression.

The barman looked across in steadied wonder until Charlie steered him to the other side of the bar with talk about a possible deal on a second hand car.

"Well, I just thought you'd like to know what has happened. We shall overlook the last minute change of venue which took place. When we arrived there were sixteen very injured men lying on the ground, which I am sure you know nothing about."

Victor could have given a corny 'I nothing about this guv, honest' style of answer but he thought that inappropriate. Instead he just raised his shoulders and mumbled something completely inaudible.

"Alright, that's not important because I'm sure you all went straight home after handing the videos over to them. One of their gang did however let on that they had kidnapped a member of your lot. Is that true?"

Vicki looked enquiringly at Victor, who asked,

"Can I ask what you have got them on?"

"At the moment it's child pornography, child molesting, running a child prostitution racket, as well as illegal gambling and drug trafficking. We raided their office and night club and the evidence is substantial. They will go down for a long time and will have to be looked after carefully because once the word gets out amongst her majesty's guests, well..."

"In that case," said Vicki who had decided that she could not really face a court case involving her as a rape victim, "they are lying about the kidnapping."

Victor decided to quickly change the subject.

"So, this must be a real feather in your cap then?"

"Yes, well, I have gained a few brownie points."

The atmosphere had changed, it was getting brighter, they had pulled it off.

"By the way," added Campbell, "I don't suppose you lot have heard anything on the underground grapevine about a series of break-ins in Strood?"

Victor shrugged his shoulders whilst Benjamin looked towards the ceiling and frowned.

"Oh heck, I forgot about that one."

"Apart from that one I look forward to helping the police out in the future," said Victor in a not very serious tone of voice, "Oh and by the way before you leave could you shout out something nice, just as you are going, the landlord thinks we're gangsters or something."

The two policemen shook hands with the group and moved towards the door.

"Thanks, Victor, for helping the public, we need more like you!" said Benjamin as the barman looked round and smiled.

'Not that bloody positive!' thought Victor.

A round of drinks appeared from the barman who resumed his usual position just by the bar chatting to another regular. Charlie joined the Class just as the music started. The first stripper moved onto the stage and started to dance. She wasn't very good. Catherine popped her head around the side door and whispered to the group in the corner,

"Don't worry lads. I'm on next."